Patrick Holloway is an Irish writer of fiction and poetry and is an editor of the literary journal, The Four Faced Liar. He completed his Masters in Creative Writing from the University of Glasgow, before moving to Porto Alegre, Brazil, where he completed his PhD in Creative Writing.

He is the winner of the Bath Short Story Award, The Molly Keane Creative Writing Prize, The Flash 500 Prize, the Allingham Fiction contest and he was the recipient of the Paul McVeigh Residency in 2023. His work appears in The Stinging Fly, The London Magazine, Poetry Ireland, The Moth, Southword, The Ilanot Review, Carve, The Irish Times and The Irish Independent.

The Language of Remembering is Patrick's debut novel.

'Holloway is a rare and immense talent. The Language of Remembering is full of the grit and texture and sweetness of life, the sorrow of loss, the wonderful, terrible mystery of our humanity. The characters feel real, their voices sing from the page and the writing is sublime. I loved every line of this novel, readers are going to love it too - it will soar.'

Donal Ryan, author of The Spinning Heart and From a Low and Quiet Sea, Booker Prize longlisted.

'The Language of Remembering is a deeply moving novel about the bonds between a mother and son, and how memory shapes love and loss. When Oisín reconnects with his mother, Brigid, he finds himself piecing together the fragments of her past, and Holloway's writing tenderly weaves seamlessly through her history. A beautiful meditation on family, love, and the fragility of remembering - this novel is a testament to the enduring power of compassion and care.'

Elaine Feeney, author of How to Build a Boat, Booker Prize longlisted.

'Tender and humane, this is a novel that examines the stuff lives are made of: language, love, memory. A lyrical and open-hearted debut.'

Seán Hewitt, author of Tongues of Fire and All Down Darkness Wide.

'In a profoundly moving tale, Holloway brings us close to real, earthy, honest, human beings whose experience comes from several languages and who live through the day-to-day minutiae of both past and present. The prose is exquisite, energetic and exciting. One of the most beautiful books you will read this year.'

Mary O'Donnell, author of The Elysium Testament and Where They Lie.

'The Language of Remembering is such a powerful, original debut, beautifully considered and crafted, full of feeling and humanity. Patrick Holloway is one of the most exciting voices to emerge in Irish writing in quite some time, and I have no doubt that this novel will bring him a wide and enthusiastic audience.'

Billy O'Callaghan, author of The Paper Man.

'The Language of Remembering is a deeply moving novel, as skilful as contemporary fiction gets. An insightful rendition of young families in the past and present day, it illuminates the sorrows and the joys that we inherit from our parents and the absences which freight our adult lives.'

Benjamin Wood, author of The Young Accomplice.

'This novel captured my heart. A devastatingly beautiful testament to the power of family, language and love. An exquisite, sharply observed story of hope and resilience. Hard to believe it's a debut!'

Danielle McLaughlin, author of The Art of Falling.

The Language of Remembering

Patrick Holloway

épuque press

Published by Epoque Press in 2025

Copyright © Patrick Holloway, 2024
All rights reserved.

The right of Patrick Holloway to be identified as the author of this work has been asserted in accordance with section 77 of the Copyright, Designs and Patents Act 1988

This book is sold subject to the condition that it shall not, by way of trade or otherwise, be lent, resold, hired out or otherwise circulated without the publisher's prior consent in any form of binding or cover other than in which it is published and without a similar condition including this condition being imposed on the subsequent purchaser.

Typeset in EB Garamond Regular, EB Garamond Regular Italic & PF Martlet Black.
Typesetting & cover design by Ten Storeys®

Printed and bound in Great Britain by
Clays Ltd, Elcograf S.p.A.

British Library Cataloguing-in-Publication Data
A catalogue record for this book is available from the British Library

ISBN 978-1-7391-881-9-1 (paperback edition)

'Love set you going like a fat watch.
The midwife slapped your footsoles, and your bald cry
Took its place among the elements.'

Sylvia Plath
'Morning Song'

'The hardest thing in this world is to live in it.'

Buffy Summers
'Buffy the Vampire Slayer'

For my parents, who never told me not to.

The Language of Remembering

Now

Cork airport is quiet. After São Paulo and Amsterdam, it is welcoming. You are exhausted from cattle class and from Ailish who couldn't settle, who cried when you said there was no room for her on your lap. Then you had to push one leg into the aisle and the other under the seat so she could lay on top of you, that way the other passengers would stop looking at her wailing, and there she sprawled for the eleven-hour flight. You focus on all the bags coming out on the carousel to keep yourself awake, hoping all eight of yours arrive. Then there's the buggy and the baby seat. You turn around to see if Nina is coming out of the toilets but there is a queue. She's tired and pissed off – the man in customs questioned her a little too much, told you to be quiet and let her answer herself. He looked at her Brazilian passport as if it were fake; held it as if it were covered in shit. He looked from the passport photo to her, to the photo, to her, to the photo, to her, each time scrunching his face a little tighter before stamping the passport and waving her on. This must be the fucking highlight of his day, smug prick.

You wondered what he thought when he saw the blue passport. Did images of favelas and guns come to his mind? Did he look upon you both as some kind of scam? You judged him quickly and then remembered when you first met Nina, the way her eyes looked down as she said, Carolina is my name and I am from Brazil. It is a little joke between you now – Carolina is my name. You remember being surprised by the vastness of what being from Brazil meant, the gaping holes in your understanding of the world. You could not even conjure up an image of what Brazil was, except knowing they were good at football, and even at that you weren't really sure. You could never have imagined the size, or that you'd end up there, in a city they considered small that you considered enormous. How green the streets were, how full of trees, full of life.

Waiting for the suitcases you think of what you've left behind. You picture your apartment, the L shaped Togo sofa, the floor to ceiling windows overlooking Parcão, and beyond it, the port. You remember the evenings – the sun splitting itself into a lunatic of gold as it glittered across the water, staining the sky mandarin. You picture yourself crossing the street, going down the hill towards your favourite açaí spot. On the right, between high buildings is the open, outdoor food hall. With stalls of churrasco, crepes, ice cream. The tanned bodies, the loudness. The buzz everywhere, all the time, alive. The feeling comes over you as the first suitcase makes its appearance. That word for which there is no translation – saudades. A longing, a stretching of missing something, someone, someplace.

You take the first suitcase off the carousel. Each one has a multicoloured label, and on it, in lovely, curvy Nina writing, is your name and the address of the house you have rented. The house you have not seen yet in person. You start taking the suitcases off, hoping they will all fit on two trolleys. Nina comes back and Ailish is in her arms, nested. You have six out of eight suitcases. The others come quick enough and you manage, with quite a lot of hassle, to arrange them on the two trolleys. You wait for the buggy and the baby seat. The last of the bags clatter to the carousel and the people head off.

There is that certain tiredness that has taken control of you. You look around without taking anything in. You know you will forget all this; in a few weeks you will remember something about the buggy but not any of the details. Nina is still standing, swaying back and forth, her eyes half open, with Ailish asleep in her arms. You go over to lost luggage and start the spiel about the missing buggy and baby chair before the woman points behind you to oversized baggage where your buggy and baby chair wait. Walking back, you cannot remember a single thing about what the woman looks like.

In the arrivals lounge, Fiona and Brian are waiting for you. Fiona is giddy and skips to you. Her hug is tight and warm, and she smells the same as she did when you were teenagers, in her parents' sitting room playing the PlayStation and talking of your insecurities. Brian hugs you too and asks about the flights. You yawn and say some hollow words. He helps you with one of the trollies. Fiona is talking to Nina and stroking Ailish's hair. You want to be more alive for the reunion, it has been too long since you've seen them, but your brain refuses to obey.

You go in the car with Brian and most of the bags; Nina and Ailish go in the other car with Fiona. The car is fancy and has leather seats and soon is toasty. Brian asks about the move, about how you're feeling, and you try not to, but before you are at the airport roundabout, you are asleep. You wake with his hand on your shoulder, shaking you.

You are bamboozled. By his hand, by the car, by the lack of sound. Your eyes take in the house beyond the windscreen, and it reminds you of a house you visited as a child. Within seconds everything jigsaws back into place and you realise it is the house you will rent. The other houses line the street, twins, triplets, quintuplets. A dolefulness comes over you and you try to smile at Brian, apologise for falling asleep, and open the door to that south-westerly wind. It's fucking freezing.

Inside, in the kitchen, once you have lined the suitcases against the wall, and Nina has gone upstairs to put Ailish into bed, the four of you sit around the small, flimsy wooden table. The kitchen is old and there is a smell of lemony cleaning products, but beneath that there is a smell of chipper food. It reminds you of the smell from your hair and hands when you used to clean plates in the Moonduster's kitchen. Smoking fags on a quick break next to the large wheelie bins, with Kate, the chef. You'd suck back the nicotine and she'd talk to you like an adult even though you were fifteen. Then back in the kitchen, loading dirty plates into the big dishwashers, you'd often have to slip your hand in your pants to tuck your boner against the elastic of your boxers. Everything made you horny back then. Even Kate, the middle-aged chef with teeth stained the colour of sand.

'Well, is it?'

Fiona is looking at you, smiling away.

'Is it what?'

'Good, is it good to be back?'

'Oh, of course. I mean, it's weird, to be honest. I'm so fucking tired I could be anywhere.'

You think of this friendship, this important relationship in your life, nearly twenty years of knowing each other inside out, and yet now, at the bockety table, you can't take it in, it means nothing; or its meaning is beyond you.

'Come on, Fio, let's leave them get a bit of sleep.' Brian is standing up and this movement makes you happy.

'No lads, stay. There's no bothers,' you say, but already Fiona is standing and so are you. Nina is the last to get up, she too was elsewhere. At the front door you all hug each other and words are said. You close the door and Nina puts her hand in yours and pulls you towards the stairs.

'What about the suitcases?' you ask now in Portuguese.

'Leave them.' You follow her upstairs and she takes a right and leads you into your new bedroom. Its size offends you immediately. The bed is worn looking and doesn't seem to want either of you there. The lampshade that hangs from the ceiling is dark olive, and you think it probably started off as a nice lime; the light from beneath it is sad.

'God, it's fucking horrific.'

'It's not so bad.'

You both sit on the bed next to each other. You bounce up and down, pushing your bum against the mattress.

'What's Ailish's room like?' you ask. It is strange to hear Portuguese float around this little Carrigaline room.

'It's fine, the ceiling slants, *eu bati* my head off it. How would I say that in English, hit?'

'Yeah, hit, smacked, whacked.'

'Whacked?'

'Yeah. I whacked my head off it.'

'Whacked. Sounds right.'

'I'm fucking wrecked.'

'Me too. I need to brush my teeth, though. All that is in the small suitcase, isn't it?'

'No idea. I'm just gonna sleep.'

'Without brushing your teeth, *que nojo*. How would I say that, disgusting?'

'Yeah, or minging. Minging is better.'

'Well, I'm going to brush my teeth, you minging.'

'I'd be a minger, something's minging, someone is a minger. I'll probably be asleep when you get back.'

'Ok, night you minger. *Te amo.*'

She closes the door with the smallest of clicks, and you realise the bedroom isn't an ensuite. You lie on the pillows and close your eyes and expect to fall asleep within seconds. Instead, your brain goes into overdrive annoyingly fast so that it gives you only moments to worry about something before replacing it with something else. The climate. The house. Nina fitting in. Ailish fitting in. You fitting back in. Jobs. A mortgage. Your mum.

You open your eyes. You haven't called her, you said you would. You check the time and it is nearly ten. What time does she sleep now? You start to send her a WhatsApp but remember the nurse said they only confuse her, that calling is better. You imagine her alone in that little house, the one she never moved from. You decide not to call, in case you wake her, in case she gets out from the bed to answer the phone and falls, maybe, or gets confused in the middle of the night and cannot get back to sleep.

You are still awake when Nina climbs in under the blanket. You reach out to her and she slides up against you. Her hands are cold, the rest of her is clothed.

'I don't know how you sleep with socks on.'

'It's freezing, I don't know how you can sleep without them. I thought you'd be asleep.'

'Couldn't.'

She taps the side of your face with her fingers, then your temples, then she pushes her hands softly through your hair.

'Always so busy up here,' and she kisses your forehead, nose, lips. She nuzzles into you and turns around so she is wrapped in your arms and within seconds her breathing becomes heavy and she is gone. You force your mind to quieten and just think of the day ahead. You'll have to go to Dunnes. You think of Barry's tea and Dairygold butter and you feel warm. Sensations from your past fill you up and you think that there should be a word for this very feeling, the one that sneaks up on you and is then everywhere, for when you come back to a place that was once your home and it still holds something of you and returns it slowly, achingly.

You close your eyes again and remember breakfasts at home when you were a child. Your mother would wake you, walking into your bedroom singing. She'd whip open the curtains and laugh at your complaints. Oh, my darling boy, she'd say as she lifted you out of bed. My darling, darling boy. Coco Pops were on the table downstairs, and your dad sat with his legs crossed, reading the newspaper. When you sat down, he'd fold the newspaper away noisily and be all yours – that lovely pocket of time it'd be just you and him while your mum got ready in the bedroom. Time alone with him had different rules.

He'd ask about your dreams and if you couldn't remember them, you'd make something up. Dragons, he'd say, well, only the bravest dream of dragons. Or, fairies, well, Ireland is the land of the fairies, they were here long before us. He'd walk your imagination along different paths, sneaking in more adventures for the nights to come. He'd tell you that he loved you. Every morning, when your mum came in to bring you to school, he'd stand you before him, put his hands on your shoulders and say, Oisín, I love you and don't ever forget it. You'd hug him and he'd hug you and even now there aren't many feelings that can beat whatever it was you felt there, then, in his arms with the day ahead of you, waiting.

You fall asleep and when you wake you remember dreaming of him. It is complete but by the time you shower and go downstairs it is gone and you spend the morning trying to remember. In that dream you are with him in a wood and there is so much brightness you have to squint when you look up at him. There are all different birds singing, squawking, croaking and cawing. And your feet are squelching in mud and it gets dark quickly and you can't find him. You can hear him a little way away but in each direction he is not there. You keep walking and in a clearing he is sitting on a bench waiting for you. You walk to him but never seem to get any closer. His arms reach out for you. He looks up and you follow his gaze and the sky, greyed by clouds, is full of little finches, golden and maple and autumn-leaved, and they fly so beautifully and freely.

Then

Brigid opened the curtains and the sun outside was nervously making its way into the sky, and the clouds shifted slightly in a separation that made her feel like there wasn't a thing to be done to stop what was coming. She tried to think of a word for how the clouds split. Whenever she couldn't come up with something, she tried to hear her mother's voice. A something separation, nervous, no, foreboding, better, but no. She closed her eyes and imagined her mother standing behind her. Deleterious. A deleterious separation.

The grass in the garden, hidden by a low mist, irritated her. The thought of the day ahead gave rise to an acute anger that came out of her in a forced sigh. She thought of all the times James told her it would be ok, that they were safe, careful. She thought of all the times she let the need for him take over, the want of wanting to be desired. And the moments afterwards.

Her hands pushed at her belly roughly. She wondered about the cells growing inside her. That's all it was now, anyway, just cells, she thought. She wanted to put in Kelly Marie's new cassette. She'd rewind it over and over and listen to *Feels Like I'm in Love*, wondering if she too felt that way. Brigid's feet felt very firmly on the ground, though. She couldn't play music yet anyway; it was too early. She dragged her body, which didn't feel much like her body, from the window in her room. The floorboards creaked and she was afraid she'd wake her parents in the room opposite, still asleep, safe from the ineluctable day that awaited. She liked that word, ineluctable. She had stolen it from her mother. She closed her eyes and each time she opened them, the ceiling seemed to have lowered a little. The dark oak wardrobe inched closer. The thick dirtied-white carpet rose to meet her. She looks at the clothes she had worn yesterday, folded neatly on her chair by her desk, willing herself to put them on. Instead, she picked up a dressing gown and tied it around herself and went to the bathroom.

She took deep breaths in front of the thin timber-framed mirror. The cold air went through her, she shivered, and her reflection trembled. Everything was so severe. The sharp angles of the mirror, the wooden cabinet next to the toilet with shampoo and packets of soap. Her thoughts too were cutting. She knew now that there must be something wrong with her. Over the last few weeks, a distinct new feeling had been born within her and it was directed at James and the baby inside of her. Abominate. Abomination. She said the word aloud and it too sounded like another word. She played with that other almost word in her head, rolling it over, weighing it up – the split futures it held. She heard her mother cough from the other room and the thought of telling her creeped like a cockroach.

Her mother never went to university and although she never spoke in what ifs, she did talk frequently about classrooms and respect for knowledge. The beauty of words, the power of them. And when she did speak like this, after the odd whiskey and water, Brigid would feel that somehow she herself was to blame for a future that never happened. For the conversation always circled around the gift of being a mother, though often the word gift sounded like something else.

Her father would be waking soon so she crept down the carpeted stairs and into the kitchen, which was even colder than the rest of the house. She looked out the back door and could see the two dogs curled into each other, sleeping under the roof of the shed. She bent down under the kitchen sink to take a pot and then filled it with the water from the tap that chugged a little before spluttering. She took the matches from the shelf above the stove and lit one of the hobs and the flames flung themselves outwards and upwards to meet the cool metal. For a second, she wanted to put her hand in the open flame, but it was a quick fanciful thought. She'd have tea waiting for her da.

Her da, Tommy, was a taciturn man but when he spoke people straightened to listen. And he only spoke Irish at home. And she only ever answered in Irish. With her mother, Kathleen, it was different. Kathleen only sang lullabies in Irish and Brigid never really knew if her mother knew the meaning of the words or not. When Tommy spoke, his words always said more than what they were saying, at least to Brigid. The way they rolled off his tongue when he was angry, like they had weight, she could hear them thud to the ground. Or no weight at all when he'd be after a pint, the way they'd float out of him, and she'd look up to see if they were trapped there among the wooden beams that triangled into the apex of the ceiling.

The water was boiling, bubbles hissing over the pot, so she grabbed the handle and moved it onto the other hob. She took two mugs down from the wooden cupboard. It was once painted a kind of olive green but now had peeled and faded into the colour of the grass where her dogs pissed. Her father had chosen the paint down at Danny's hardware store, the exact hue of it her mother had called meretricious, and her father said go on away with your metericious. Her mother had laughed and left him to his painting and he'd turned and looked down at Brigid and shrugged his shoulders before fighting a little with the opening of the lid.

Kathleen read vivaciously. Brigid's grandfather, whom she had never met, had taught Kathleen to read and told her she should go to college, even though no girl from Minane Bridge had ever gone to college. He used to buy her books upon books, which she left all over the house so there was nowhere she could not read. He told her that she was destined for illustriousness, and later that night she checked her dictionary to see what it meant and smiled into her pillow.

Brigid put the round tea into the straining spoon and splashed the water in, took the dewy glass bottle of milk from the fridge and smelled it before pouring a little in each mug. She felt a little weak, queasy down below. Was it taking something from her already? Draining her of a future? She cut a slice of the loaf that was hardening at the crust and spread some butter and the blackberry jam and ate it without thinking about the fact that she was eating. She strained the tea, squeezing at the handles of the spoon until the milky tint turned earthy. She always marvelled at how it leaked a new colour, how it became something different in the time it took to filter the loose-leaf tea. She heard her dad rise above, the wooden floorboards creaking. She ran to the back door, opened it and wretched right there on the doorstep. The dogs tilted their heads and shook their lazy bodies to rise up, then stretched their front legs and scurried over to see what was at her feet.

She wanted to wash the puke away before her dad got down the stairs. The dogs were already sniffing at it, tongues at the ready. She walked to the hose at the side of the house. Her hands felt the chill of the tap and she could feel the icy water surge through. The dogs scattered as she put her thumb against the hole to spray the puke this way and that. It was as if already her body was not her own. It wanted to rid itself of something, but she couldn't give a name to it. When she looked up her dad was in the kitchen, looking out.

She turned off the hose and the dogs were back by the door, sniffing for the leftovers. Inside, Tommy was at the table with his tea. She felt bubbles inside of her rising up, and her mind sprawled words around as she tried to hold onto the last nerves of equanimity.

'One of the dogs made a mess?' He asked, as Gaeilge.

'Yeah,' she said, 'there's something up with one of them anyway. They're grand out there now.'

He sipped at his tea and she took her mug and sat down next to him.

'Is mum up?'

'Not up,' he said, 'but awake, she's reading up there.'

'What's new?'

He didn't answer but instead nodded. They sat and slurped the tea without saying much else and it suited Brigid just fine. He got up and walked to the front door, bringing in a glass bottle of milk in one hand, still wet with condensation, and The Irish Independent in the other. He sat back down and ruffled the paper. She tried to feel the chair beneath her, the heat from the mug. Something would have to be done, she just didn't have the faintest idea what. She looked at him and wondered what the news would do to him. How she would find words to tell him. Did the words exist? Could they be put together in a way that made sense? Could she maybe mix Irish and English to find the perfect rhythm? She took the empty mugs from the table to the sink. Her father's voice was low and she felt it make its way towards her, creeping up her legs and climbing her back.

'Well, he's well and truly in now anyway.' Her dad said, closing the newspaper.

'Who?'

'Carter. I think he might actually do some good.'

'Sure it won't change much here.'

'You'd be surprised. And herself will be 25 years on the throne next week.'

'One of the teachers was saying there's plans of her visiting up north.'

'Well, I'd love to see the Falls Road if she does. You seeing James today?'

'I am. After work. I get off at three.'

'Right so,' he said as she put the mugs on the tea towel next to the sink to dry. Her dad got up to cut some of the loaf.

'There's not long left in it,' she said.

'Sure your mother will find some use for it.'

She moved past him and thought he looked at her askance, but she kept walking and told him she'd better shower before work. He said to not be in there too long, there's not much hot water to be had, and she told him not to worry, she'd be quick, sure she didn't need to wash her hair. She looked at him from the door, his face with dawn's stubble, his rough hands buttering the bread, his hair flopping slightly, greying now. For the first time he looked frail to her, fracturable.

Walking up the stairs she thought of James. The words formed on her tongue, the tone she tried to hear in the depths of her mind. She knew she'd have to control herself and not throw the words at him, but let them whisper, caress. Reaching the top of the stairs, Kathleen asked her to come in. She was propped up against two pillows with a cigarette in one hand and the other holding yesterday's Irish Times. Tommy's side was empty of blankets and pillows and Brigid lay down next to her.

'Loyalty and friendship, they're saying, 25 years of it supposedly,' said her mother without looking at Brigid.

'The queen, is it?'

'Loyalty and friendship, come off it. If it's a euphemism, it's a weak one at best. Silly woman is what she is, the whole lot of them playing bloody dress up.'

Brigid didn't answer and Kathleen looked at her, folding away the paper.

'What's got into you?'

'Nothing. What do you mean?'

'I'm the one asking you! You're looking, well, you're looking a little blanched.'

'Blanched?'

'Yes, blanched, Brigid, blanched. It means pale. You don't look well is what I mean.' She blew smoke from the side of her mouth, away from Brigid.

'I'm grand. I just didn't sleep well.'

Already Brigid felt flushed. She could picture the little red dots dancing across her face, joining up and ceilidhing down her neck and shoulders. How would the days keep on? How would the sun just go on rising languidly and setting the way it does, gradually and then all at once? She thought of telling Deidre at the cafe where she worked, her disappointed face saying she'd have to let her go. Thought of James' parents, their messianic mouths agape. Her Da. His words bricky and sharp, or the silence that would steam from him. She thought of Father McCarthy, what he'd say to her, to her parents. Her teachers, Ms. Murphy, who told her she had a beautiful brain and a lovely way with words. Who once gave her a lift home and gifted her novels she thought she'd like and told her she should already be thinking about her future, because if she played it right, she could be very special. Her friends, who surely would gossip. Rob from the local shop who was always nice to her and sometimes gave her his homemade jam, the jar all wrapped in lovely crisp paper. Her friends' parents. The postman, who always had a quick cup of tea out the back. They all seemed to become too many and too big in her mind.

She tilted her head to look up at her mother, who was scrunching her lips to one side of her mouth – a wry, weighty guise. She had the talent to do that, to change the whole look upon her face by moving one side of her mouth slightly, or by creasing the corner of her eye; she had the ability to put into words what Brigid was feeling with the slightest of movements.

'Well,' Kathleen said, putting out the cigarette in the ashtray on her bedside locker, getting out of bed and, with a slight turn of her hand, gesturing for Brigid to do the same, 'what a quandary.' Brigid couldn't tell if Kathleen was angry when she walked round the side of the bed and took tufts of Brigid's hair, smoothing them out between her fingers.

Brigid wanted to ask her mother what she felt when she found out. What future she had all painted and framed in her mind. But she didn't ask because she already knew and did not want to hear the firmness of truth, because if Brigid were to ask, Kathleen would give it to her straight.

Outside, the sun had declared all of itself to the sky. Brigid wanted to say something, or for her mother to say something, for it to be spoken. For the words to meet the air. Wanted to hear how the word sounded, the magnitude of it. But her mother let her go and said to get a move on or she'd be late for work. And when Brigid went into her room to get ready, she wondered if her mother actually knew at all.

In the shower she thought of the word blanched, and quandary. How she could use them later when speaking to James. She thought of the year and a half they'd been together. First kissing outside a disco in the community centre. She remembered how she opened her eyes to see if anyone was looking. Sure all the girls fancied him, and all the boys were always a step behind him, waiting for him to decide what to do next. He was the best soccer player in town and on match days people from across the bridge and even a few men from the city used to come out and watch. There was talk of him joining all kinds of teams. A hype in the air around him.

He told her he had no interest in playing soccer but there was a look that came over him after matches, or when there was talk about scouts coming to watch. She knew he enjoyed the attention of it. Sure, that would be the end of us, she would say, with you going to England to be the big fancy star that you are. He'd laugh at her and say that it would never happen.

'It would be better than shoving my arms into heifers, though. Hours it fucking takes,' he'd told her, 'and your arms would be ruined after. Jesus. Then the placenta passes. I'm telling you Bridge, it's brutal.'

He was well able to change the conversation when he wanted to. He made every day seem new, like it was the first. An excitement to him that was hard to tame. The first time he told her he wrote poetry she laughed out and said to go on away. Then he looked down and it took him a while to lift his head back up and catch her eye. He had never shown anyone apart from her and she'd asked him so many times if she could show her mammy.

'She'd love them, I know she would. They're brilliant James.'

'Ara.'

'No, really they are.'

He'd smile then and say, 'well I have another one written.'

He'd always take his time reading them. Sometimes she'd want to interrupt and say, come on, get on with it, but she loved how he teased out the words, too. The music of them. After it, there'd be something different in the air, something seraphic.

They'd been quick about most things. Kissing, saying I love you, introducing each other to their parents, and riding. That's what James called it and Brigid laughed. How different the word sounded when he was joking around and how fascinating and other-worldly it sounded the moment just after. There was nothing romantic about it – normally it was done in one of the warehouses on his dad's farm or in the back of a trailer. She'd worried, of course, about the possibility, but he had always calmed her. Showed her each time how delicate he was putting on the Frenchie. He'd got a load from his cousin who had been back from England the summer before. As they started running out, though, the fear rose in both of them.

As soon as they had no more left, Brigid had started counting the days between her cycle, writing it all down in the back of her copybook. She'd count and count again. She could never really trust the Billings method, sure hadn't a girl over the bridge got pregnant only last year and Brigid's classmate, who was the girl's cousin, had told her she'd been doing the method and couldn't believe it when she found out. For a while now, Brigid had been thinking about going to the young doctor in the city. She'd die if she had to go to the family doctor, who knew her mother so well. But that new doctor was meant to be great. She'd seen him once down the village, leaving the chemist one morning. He had his hair down to his neck and used his hand to brush through it, bringing it out of his eyes. She'd even made up the excuse to go – a terrible pain in her jaw, and it'd clack during the night so she couldn't sleep. How she'd ever even bring up the pill was beyond her, but she'd been months now, trying to build up the courage.

They'd stopped the riding in spurts because the fear became too much altogether. Sometimes, right after, when she was enjoying being in his arms and the warmth still inside her, she'd imagine the worst. There were morsels of truth she had not even told herself yet. The dreams she had. They'd come to her in fragmented images. Her standing in a lecture hall, looking out on hands shot upright into the air. Or sitting in a venerable, high-ceilinged room, coffee on the table, and colleagues with books open on their laps, a buzz of conversations. She could hear heels click on the city pavements.

'Imagine,' she'd said to James, 'if something were to happen, and the whole village knowing we were at it.'

'It'd kill my mother,' he had said, and Brigid scoffed.

'What?' he said, 'it would.'

'Oh, your poor mother. I'd be to blame anyway, I'd be the slut. Not much would change for you, it'd be me they'd all be gawping at, me who'd be the brazen one. You'd still be off playing soccer and doing whatever it is ye do afterwards.'

'Ah, Bridge, I didn't mean it, I was just saying. And look, it's not going to happen anyway, sure we're not even at it anymore.'

But the bouts never lasted long. She surprised herself at relishing the danger of it, not just the act, but the secrecy to it all. The excuses they would make to chisel time for themselves.

Then, later, being back with her friends, or at home with her parents, with this delicious secret breathing inside of her.

She dried herself and put on her clothes. She brushed her hair quickly and tied it up tight. In the hall she called to her mother that she'd be off and she'd be back late because she was meeting James after work.

'Just make sure you're back for dinner.'

'I will,' she said, and held the banister as she walked down the stairs. At the front door she shouted into her dad.

'Bhuel, táim ag imeacht.'

'Lean ort, maith thú' he shouted, and she closed the door behind her.

The cold air was brilliant on her breath and she walked around the corner with the road unchanged beneath her feet. As soon as her house was out of sight, she took matches and a cigarette out from her bag, cupped her hands to light the match and brought it up to the cigarette in her mouth. The first inhale was lovely and the smoke left her mouth all thick and full of knowing, fading into the unseen air. She didn't pass many people and the few she did just waved or nodded at her and went on about their day. How different that'll be, she thought. She didn't know if she'd be able to handle the whispering, the silence when she'd enter a room, the judging, probably from her friends, too. They'd all make out like they weren't doing the exact same thing. The word brazen kept coming back to her. By the time she reached the bus stop her heart was racing, and on the bus, all the way down to Crosshaven, she imagined herself on the same bus a few months down the line, how she'd sit there at all. By the time she got off and walked over to the cafe she was all flustered and had to go to the bathroom to splash water on her face, before putting on her apron and going out to take the first orders of the day.

Now

The first week in the house is spent calling phone companies, organising Personal Public Service numbers, and trying to find the cheapest insurance for the second-hand car you bought on a whim. The first two days you had to wait for buses that were always late. It was strange being on a bus again, it brought back memories you hadn't thought of in years. The burn after swigs from a Smirnoff naggin, before passing it on to Fiona or Eoin. Risking going into town, worried you wouldn't be allowed in anywhere for you were shorter than your friends and your face was soft and smooth, not a hair in sight. After two days of riding the bus, with its moquette carpeted chairs, you called Fiona who brought you into town and dropped you off at a second-hand car dealership where you spoke to a salesman called Paul, who reminded you of the dad from Matilda. He kept putting his hands in his pockets only to take them straight out again. You started counting how many times he did it. He showed you three cars – a Peugeot, a Skoda and a Nissan. You didn't really like any but the Skoda had internal lights on the dashboard and on the sides of the doors that you could change the colour of. Ailish would love that, so you offered him four grand less to which he laughed at, before slowly bargaining a sale. You drove it home uninsured, and Nina raised her hands up to the sky as you parked in the driveway.

Every time you thought of visiting your mum, you found something else to do. You had to buy wheelie bins, a lawnmower, warmer clothes for Ailish. On the eighth day, Nina wakes you up. It is still dark outside and you're not sure what time it is. It's warm under the blankets and she puts her leg in between yours. The heat off her does things to you. She kisses your mouth.

'I wouldn't,' you say, and wipe at the dry saliva stuck to your lips.

She kisses your chin, your neck. You haven't had sex since you arrived. There is an urgency to it. You both want it to last but also want it uninterrupted, so it is brisk, a little in fast forward, and more for you than for her.

'Do you want me to?' You ask, your hand going back down. She lies into the pillow so your hand is at an awkward angle, but you don't want to break the rhythm. Afterwards, she is smiling and turns to you.

'I think we're going to be fine, here, you know?' Her eyes are still only half open.

'Good, me too.'

'Really?'

'Yeah, why?'

'I don't know, you've been weird, like a little heavy or something. And you haven't visited your mum.'

'It's just been busy.'

You turn around and get up, already odd at yourself for

avoiding the conversation. In the bathroom you think maybe she's been trying to approach this for a while. Probably the sex was an inroad. Every time you avoid a conversation or get odd and start a little argument over nothing, you can see the childishness of it and know you're being a dick and think it will be the last time, but time and time again you avoid.

She waddles in, cupping toilet paper between her legs. You want to say sorry, want to tell her you're afraid of seeing your mum again, afraid she won't know who you are, but instead you turn off the tap and leave. You go downstairs, avoiding the third stair which creaks and wakes Ailish. The light switch for the kitchen is on the wall behind the door, which irritates the fuck out of you. The kitchen is beige, and the cupboards are old pine, and it looks like a thousand other kitchens. You boil the kettle, a marzipan colour that doesn't show where the water level is at anymore. You use the French press to make coffee and have two mugs ready for when Nina comes down.

She is in her pyjamas and a thick dressing gown. You put the mugs on the kitchen table that has a horrendous checkered tablecloth – it looks like a giant Battenberg cake.

'Thanks,' she says, not catching your eye. You sit down next to her.

'I'm going to visit my mum today. I should also really look for a job, I was chatting to the lads about a mortgage, and they said we've fuck all hope with the money coming in from Brazil.'

'That's good. About your mum, I mean. Not about the mortgage. What would you look for?'

You don't answer because you don't really know. A decade spent in Brazil, where you worked as a consultant for different companies. Basically, you were a glorified simultaneous translator. You started in one meeting for a law firm and had a drink with the lawyer afterwards. Then, within a month, he had recommended you to more people, then them to more people, and soon you were in demand. You enjoyed it most of the time because it was just chatting really, simplifying what one person said so the other could understand it. You took joy from seeing conversations move forward because of you. For people to understand one another through you. At times it made you feel powerful. The way they looked at you. You knew the weight of your words, the nuance between choosing one verb over another, the effect of using a colloquial expression or not. It came so easy to you, Portuguese. Like it had always been there, inside, waiting to fall out of you.

'I think it'll be hard for me to find something. I don't really have a job title.'

'But you think it'll be easier for me?'

'It'll definitely be easier for you, you work in HR, but that's not what I was implying – don't worry, you don't have to find anything.'

You get up, annoyed that she thought you were hinting at her getting a job, when really that's exactly what you were doing. You just want a mortgage and a nice house and a view of the sea. You feel poor, and after years of not being poor you worry what it will do to you. Since you've moved back you've felt the need to justify everything to your friends and people you meet on the street; feel that they are thinking you've fallen from a height, have failed in some way by moving home. That is what it is like to live in a village – a small army you have to please, a troop of people you barely know yet somehow seek their admiration.

You go back and sit at the table.

'Sorry, I'm being a dick.'

'It's ok. I know things are stressful.'

'Yeah but like, they're harder for you, I know you miss your parents. It's just – I just feel like I've moved us here and maybe things will take forever to fall into place.'

'You moved us here? We moved here.'

'I know. You know what I mean.'

'You need to give yourself a break, we've been here like a week.'

'I know.'

She reaches over and squeezes your shoulder. Ailish wakes upstairs and you go up to change her nappy. That's another thing, you think, that you have to do – check to see when she should stop using nappies at night, maybe she's late. With the stress of the move, you both have given her liberties. She is sitting up in her bed when you open the door.

'Papai!' She shuffles off the bed and climbs into your arms. Her cheek is warm against yours. She looks at you, pulling your face down from the temples.

'Papai happy?' She is already mixing the languages, starting to favour English.

'Of course, smoocher. Did you dream?' you ask in Portuguese.

'Sim!'

'Of what?'

'Dragons!'

'Dragões? Were they good or bad?'

She just smiles and puts her head back onto your shoulder. You lay her on the bed and take her pyjamas off. Get the baby wipes and Sudocream. She sings songs under her breath while you change her. You choose a long-sleeved dress for her. Tie her hair up in a ponytail.

'Let's see Birdy today?'

She doesn't answer. She calls your mother Birdy because there was no way your mother would allow for grandma or granny and certainly not nanny, and Ailish couldn't pronounce Brigid so instead she became Birdy. You feel the name has lost its power over her. Over the last year the video calls have lessened, and you are guilty of not bringing her up in conversation. You used to show Ailish photos of her but it became difficult for you. Being so far away. Now you are back it seems even more difficult. Knowing that there is something you can do is harder, still. You wonder if you should take Ailish at all.

You bring her downstairs and Nina has made scrambled eggs.

'I think I might go alone today. What do you think?'

'Yeah, I think that's better. Are you leaving now?'

'Yeah, is that ok?'

'Of course.'

She slides the eggs from the pan into Ailish's plastic, shallow bowl. She comes to you and hugs you and then Ailish is at your legs and you lift her up.

'Group hug!'

Ailish puts one arm around you and the other around Nina, and the three of you jump up and down a little until Ailish is laughing. In these moments everything is so simple. Everything is so complete that you feel absurd for stressing so much; you feel ungrateful.

You drive to Crosshaven, marvelling a little at how still the Owenabue river can be. You turn right by the yacht club, past the little fire station and up Philomena's Road. You drive to the end where the bungalow stands. It is on its last legs, you think. The paint peeling, the tiles of the roof mossy, the small patches of grass out the front are overgrown with weeds. You park outside, tap the steering wheel. Getting out, you wonder if you have to knock.

You open the door slowly and the nurse comes out of the sitting room into the hall. Her name is Mary and you have never actually met her, just spoken to her on the phone.

'You must be Oisín.' She walks over and hugs you.

'Sorry I couldn't come last week, things have been mental.'

'Oh, that's fine, that's fine. Brigid is in watching Countdown.'

Hearing her name is strange and it doesn't exactly sound like it belongs to her anymore, like that is slowly being taken, too. You walk inside and she is sitting in the armchair. The room looks so much smaller; she looks so much smaller.

'Oisín? Oisín!'

Mary is by her side although you didn't see her move past you and she is helping your mother up, but your mother pushes her away and stands up on her own. You want to move to her but stand still.

'Mum, it's me,' you say, even though she just said your name.

She looks up at you and she is still young – that surprises you. Her face is still beautiful, her cat eyes still the palest blue, wet now with tears. You hug her and she has lost weight. You feel her shudder against you. When she looks at you again, she is crying. You have seen her cry only once like this. It was not long after your father died and she took you to Curraghbinny woods.

It was cold but the sun was out and she had shoved biscuits and juice and oranges into a plastic bag and said you were going for a picnic. It's too fucking sad in here, she said. It was also one of the only times you remember your mother swearing. She parked in the little car park, and you followed her to the wooden table and benches that were bolted into the ground. The table was too far for you to reach but you didn't want to complain. She hadn't spoken a word the whole way there.

You both sat at the table. A few people walked their dogs. It was mostly quiet apart from the slight breeze that played swooshing sounds off the branches and the leaves. Your mother peeled an orange and gave you a piece. You spat out the seeds and ate it even though you weren't hungry.

'Can I go explore?' you asked, knowing she'd say no.

'Ok, but stay close,' she said without looking at you.

You walked down a little trek that opened to a larger path. The trees on both sides arched over you making a tunnel of brilliant green. Splinters of sun fell on the brown, crispy leaves. You looked up and imagined fairies flying between the branches, trying to stay hidden. Walking further, the path led you to a large open woodland, with trees further down by the sea. The ones closer to you were spread out and twisted in ghostlike shapes. A large blue rope hung down from one branch, swaying a little as if invisible hands were circling it. You wanted to walk over and touch it but didn't. You thought it was a swing but couldn't figure how it would work.

When you got back to the table your mother was crying. You saw her from behind first, her shoulders folded in, her head in her hands. You hadn't seen her cry in the act, ever, only the afters of crying. Red, puffy eyes and her face all blotchy. You didn't know if you should go to her or head back down the trail and pretend you never saw. You took a step backwards to turn away and stood on a branch and it cracked and echoed. She turned around and you walked to her, not wanting her to think you were going to leave her on her own.

You sat next to her and leaned against her soft jacket. She put her arm around you and hummed slightly, before singing in Irish. The words were at home in the woods, those words you couldn't quite grasp. They were part of the woodland, the shadows and the light. The taste of orange still in your mouth was like a feeling all of its own. You looked up again and thought you could see things move among the branches. You imagined a little audience up there, listening to your mother singing, her voice a little husky from crying. When she finished, you wanted to say something but even the silence sounded strange and beautiful and you did not want to disturb it.

Looking at her now, you wonder how you are both the same people, how this is the same life. She goes back to her armchair and you sit down on the sofa, facing her. Mary turns off the television and when you look for her she is already gone. Your mother is using the sleeve of her cardigan to wipe at her eyes.

'Where's my granddaughter?'

'Ailish, she's at home. I can bring her down this weekend.'

'And your lovely wife?'

'Nina, she's with Ailish. How are you feeling?'

'Oh, you know, good days and bad days. Sometimes I just feel lost inside myself, that's all. Obscured. Flummoxed.'

'Nothing wrong with your vocabulary anyway. How about Mary, do you like her?'

'The nurse? Oh, she's pleasant but there's no real need for her.'

'You know there is, the doctors said it was that or...'

'I know, a nursing home, dreadful places. Don't you dare put me in one. Disheartening places.'

You remember your grandmother.

'How's gran?'

'Oh, fine. Still in the sticks. Don't tell me you haven't called her.'

'I have, I have,' you lie. 'Can I get you something? Tea?'

'I'm not old you know. How about a glass of wine, there should be something in the...you'll find it anyway in there.' She uses her hand to wave you in the direction of the kitchen.

'It's a little early, mum.'

'It is not, I just had lunch.'

You find Mary sitting at the small circular table in the kitchen. The tablecloth is plastic with the pattern of flowers. You sit down next to her.

'She thinks she's had lunch. Is that normal?'

'It is, she's not great with time now. That and small things, misplacing items and stuff like that. She also gets very flustered if she has to make decisions, so most days I just decide for her, she has better days then. It must be hard for you, are you ok?'

'I'm fine, no, I'm fine. I'll make her tea. Thanks again for everything.'

You fill the kettle and look out the window that looks out on the back garden. It is a sharp slant of dead grass with a bench at the top – it is hard not to think of your father.

'She has a doctor's appointment tomorrow, if you'd like to take her.'

'Oh,' you turn and smile at her, 'yeah, I can do. What time?'

'It's in the afternoon. Two o clock, I think. I have it in my diary, I'll just check.'

She takes out a little black leather notebook from her bag, which is hanging from the chair.

'Yes, 2pm. It's in Carrigaline, in the new doctors' surgery, out by the industrial park, do you know it?'

'I don't, but sure I can use Google Maps, there's no bothers.'

'Oh great, that'll be great so.'

'Would you like a cup of tea or coffee or something?'

'I'm fine thanks, had my coffee already this morning. Ah, by the way, Kathleen called again today, she'll be coming round tomorrow, too.'

'Oh, great. Thanks a mil.'

You know your grandmother put her up to that, can almost hear her voice sculpting asides and hints. You laugh a little while making the two mugs of tea and then bring them back into the sitting room. Your mother is looking at the blank screen of the television.

'I made tea.'

'Tea? I just had some. I think the television is after surceasing.'

'Mary turned it off.'

'There was a programme I wanted to watch later, too. Oh, well.'

You ignore the comment and place the tea on the table next to her. You look around the room and remember her moving around the house with a hoover in one hand, a book in the other, knocking into side tables and the corner of the sofa. Your father laughing and saying, why don't you just put the book away, and your mother with a quick, why don't you just do the hoovering, and her laugh taking her out of the room.

'I read a great book last week, mum,' you say.

'Oh, which one? I've tried but it's beyond me now, the words, they're just...'

'I can read to you if you want.'

'Oh, no, I have a way of reading. Not sure it would be the same. I listen to the radio a lot now. There's a station that plays old Irish music early in the mornings. Reminds me of my father. You probably don't remember much of him. He simply couldn't get enough of you.'

'I remember doing jigsaws with him at the kitchen table.'

'He framed one, did you know that? You finished it in less than a minute. He said you were a prodigy.'

'I was far from a prodigy anyway.'

'You changed everything. When I think of it all now, what a wonder it was.'

She looks at you and her eyes are smiling, then she looks at the fireplace, then to the TV and slaps her hands on her knees and throws her head back, scoffing.

'Gone again, that'll cost me a fortune!'

'What, the TV? Mary turned it off, that's all.'

'Who? That one from the village, are you still with her? I thought you had more sagacity now then to still be with the likes of her.'

She is tutting and scratching her arms.

'Mary, mum, the nurse. She's in the kitchen.'

'Oh, I'm sure she is. Certain of it, in fact.'

'Mum, are you feeling alright?'

She turns and looks at you and smiles a little and reaches out to touch the side of your face.

'Mo pheata.'

The sound of Irish unsettles you.

'Come on now, you know I've no Irish, mum.'

She looks away again to the television.

'I suppose I'll have to call someone out to have a look at it. That'll be extortionate of course!'

Again, she rolls her eyes. You do not say anything but want to get up and run out of the house. The sitting room is the same as it was twenty years ago, you sit in in the same armchair, your mother sits in the same place, the windows look out on the same houses, yet everything is different, and it makes you feel nauseous. You cannot drink your tea and hope Mary will come back into the room before more of what used to be between you unravels.

'Do you want me to turn on the TV, mum?'

'Of course not. I've missed you. How is your wife?'

'Nina, she's great mum, settling in well now. I've missed you, too. I thought I could take you to your doctor's appointment tomorrow?'

'Oh, no need. I'll drive up on my own. I might see if Gwen is around, she might want to meet for a coffee.'

You smile at her. Your heart feels too large and it's in the wrong place. You remember Gwen, your mum's best friend. Remember the cancer. Remember flying home to be with your mum after the funeral. You stand up and the room again seems too small.

'Mum, I better be heading back, there's loads still to do. I'll see you tomorrow.'

She stands up and walks over to you.

'Mo pheata!'

You hug her, then, breaking away, walk out of the room and straight to the front door. You go to open it and hear Mary behind you.

'Are you off already?'

'I am yeah,' you say, without turning, your voice cracking down the middle. 'I'll be down tomorrow. Thanks Mary.'

You close the door and walk to your car with the world a darker shade of what it was before.

Then

James was waiting on the other side of the road as Brigid left the cafe. He was standing with one foot against the low wall, his arms crossed, looking beyond the sea. The tide was out and seagulls and crows swooped around the muddy waters. He hadn't seen her yet and Brigid walked slowly over to him, admiring his stature. She wanted to choose the right place, the right time to tell him. When he saw her, he smiled and pushed himself off against the wall and strode towards her. He was wearing a blue hoody and white soccer shorts. They walked by the wall, across the village, holding hands.

'How was work?' He asked, slowing his step.

'Grand. Quiet out today.'

'That Belinda is awful queer.'

'Ah, she's nice enough. Strict like, but she's grand.'

'I don't know, she's always...like, she'd always be looking at you weird.'

His eyes were a pale blue and, in summer, when he got a bit

of a tan, they shimmered inside his head. She smiled and leaned into him. They were approaching the pier and the sun was just about breaking through some of the clouds and the rays made diamonds of the water.

'Will we sit down by the pier for a bit?' she asked.

'Are you not cold?'

'I'm alright. Aren't you? Shorts on as if it was roasting.'

'Don't feel a thing, too much muscle for that.'

There were railings down by the pier and in summer they'd get the bus down and sit with their legs dangling over, watching the fishing boats go out to sea. They didn't sit now but stood facing each other. He kissed her. The wind blew in sheets across the water, rocking the boats.

'I'm pregnant James.'

He looked at her and laughed a little but the laugh died against the wind. She watched his face change, slight, dramatic movements. His eyebrows getting closer together; a biting of lips.

'How do you know? Have you been to the doctor? Was it O' Mahoney?'

'I haven't been yet.'

'Ah, come on then. Are you having me on?'

'No, James. I'm not having you on! Jesus.'

'How can you be sure? I mean we were safe.'

'Not always. I know I am. I do, I just know.'

'Come on now, how would you know? You look the exact same.'

'I know, James. I haven't had my period and I'm shattered. I just feel it, I know it.'

'Jesus Christ. Tell me this is a fucking joke!'

She moved back from him. She'd heard him use this voice after soccer matches, but never to her. The sheer force of it left

The Language of Remembering

her wordless. His teeth bit at his lips and his hands moved as if not part of his body at all but belonging to something wild and unforgiving. She waited for him to say sorry, to say something else but he didn't.

'Of course I'm not joking!'

'Fucking hell. Jesus fucking Christ.'

'Will you stop shouting at me.'

He turned his back to her, then turned to face her, before turning around again and walking away.

'What are you doing?' She shouted but her body made no effort in following him.

'Are you actually just going to walk away?'

She saw his hands shoot up in the air and, through the wind, heard him scream back, I can't fucking do it Bridge, I can't fucking do it.

She took the box of cigarettes out and lit one, blowing smoke down at her feet. The word quandary on her tongue. She started crying even though she didn't want to be crying. She sucked at the cigarette. It had seemed doable before. For some reason, the last few days she hadn't been worried. What about the future, she had thought, what of it, I'll have James and we'll make things work.

She stomped her feet and realised how childish it was but continued doing it. Stupid, she thought, I mean, so stupid, so naive. A coin had been thrown in the air, flipping and spinning and now landing in a closed fist, turned flat on top of another hand showing the other side. Whatever was there to be won, she had lost. Her eyes were sore and her cheeks were cold and she had a mad notion to throw herself into the sea to make him love her completely, so that nothing else mattered. She wanted to be saved.

The road in front of her was now incredibly long and her future, whatever still frames she had conjured up, had shattered, so when she closed her eyes all she could see was the speckled darkness. Secretly she had dreamt of university, a masters, a PhD. To lose herself in other worlds. She had gone with her class to the open day in UCC only the other week. They'd all piled onto the bus and she had sat next to James and they spoke about what they thought everyone would end up doing, trying to hear each other under the singing that came from the back of the bus. She didn't tell him about what she thought she would end up being, did not give voice to the images.

When they walked down the steps and the quad came into view she felt giddy. She stood still but her feet were tapping frantically, urging her to explore. There was a buzz she had never felt before. Clusters of students, walking hurriedly, with importance, to Brigid at least – a sense of purpose in the world around them. She found herself strolling away from her own group only to be called back by Ms. Murphy who whispered as she passed, you've not much longer to be waiting yourself now. Brigid smiled and when she reached James he asked what was all that about but Brigid just said nothing, nothing, so what do you think of it?

She could see he wasn't excited which made her want to diminish her own enthusiasm, keep it locked up. As they walked into lecture theatres, and into Boole library, she found herself thinking of her mother. From one window she could see into one of the smaller classrooms and a woman was standing at the front, and the light from the projector was shining on one side of her face, and Brigid could have sworn it was her mother. The way one hand lay on her hip and the other was out in front of her, flat, moving a little to emphasise a point.

On the bus back home she pretended to sleep on James' shoulder. She did loops of the tour again in her mind, only one time she was a student, another time she was walking to hand in her dissertation, another she was a professor and she spoke to students on her way through the halls, telling them to hurry, or asking about an assignment, and they all smiled at her and she felt respected. When the bus parked back up by the school she realised that James hadn't appeared in any of the daydreams.

She made her way for home now, her head down as the odd car passed. The wind grew stronger, a spikiness to it. She was so lost in her thoughts that she almost walked straight into Ms. Kiely who stood back and said, Brigid, slow down. Are you alright? Brigid looked at her face that had too much skin; skin drooping over more skin. Her eyes etched into her skull, little slits of yellow and green.

'What happened?'

'Nothing, thanks. I'm fine.'

'Did you argue with James? These things happen, don't be...'

Brigid walked past her, brushing against her to stay on the pavement. She kept walking. Stupid little gossiping bitch, she thought. What does she know? She never married, she never had kids. Spending her days going to fucking church. Kneeling, kneeling and more kneeling. What had she done with her life? Nothing.

It felt good to curse. She shouted the words in her mind. Stupid fucking Ms. Kiely, what does she know! She probably didn't read, apart from the bible. Fuck her, and fuck James. Her stomach tightened now, thinking of James. She hoped he was just angry, but what if he wasn't? What if she'd been wrong about the whole thing? It'd be easy for him to just leave her. To have nothing more to do with it. She saw her own future get smaller and smaller, something far off and terse and unkind.

She reached her house and went around the side and in the back door. There was nobody in the kitchen and she walked right up to her room and looked out from her window to see the road she had walked up and the village in the distance and it all seemed so insufficient. She hated it. The image of herself pushing a buggy up the road filled her with an anger. Her mother knocked on her door and came in before Brigid could answer. Brigid was still by the window looking out. Kathleen sat on Brigid's bed and didn't say anything until finally Brigid turned around, with tears in her eyes. Kathleen didn't rise to meet her but waited for Brigid to come sit next to her, and then put her arm around her and swayed side to side with her, singing in Irish. Brigid wanted to sing along. The words were all there inside her mouth, but she knew if she opened her mouth other things would come out, and she wasn't ready.

Kathleen finished singing, with her voice low, the last of the words more like whispers – Óró, sé do bheatha 'bhaile anois ar theacht an tsamhraidh. Brigid looked around her small room. Her single bed, the small table and chair with books scattered across them, and copy books with biros bitten at, and the wardrobe behind the door. There'd be no room, she thought, for a crib. She had thought about the baby in abstract, fanciful flashes. She'd be carrying him – she had decided already it was a boy – in her arms up the stairs and putting the baby boy down in a white cot, with layers like a wedding cake, in the baby's own room. Alone now, perhaps. Her body felt like somebody else's. It would ruin her. It was clear now. With or without James, it would ruin who she was, who she was going to be.

She looked at her mother now and, before asking, hoped a secret would come from her mother's lips, something that all mothers pass down to all daughters when they need it most; words that would still the loudness and bring her back to herself.

'What should I do?' Brigid asked, hearing her voice falter, and although she knew it was her own voice and it left her mouth at that moment, she also thought it could have been any woman's voice – an echo of centuries, falling hollow, defeated to the callousness of the world.

'How but in custom and in ceremony are innocence and beauty born?'

'What? What's that supposed to mean?'

'It means you need to marry, Brigid. And if I were you, I'd be quick about it, with James' parents the way they are.'

She didn't want to tell her about what happened with James, about how he walked away from her. He must not love me, she thought then, nobody who loves somebody could do that.

'But we've not finished school. I mean, I don't know he'd even want to.'

'Well, I'm sorry to be the bearer of worse news, but I don't much think either of you have a choice. I wish it were different, but for now, this is the way it is. We've no way of getting you to England and you've heard those pro-life religious, foolish fanatics since the law was passed. And besides, your father wouldn't stand for it.'

'I don't want that. I would never go to England.'

'Well then! What else is there to be done, Brigid? The answer is clear.'

'Does Da know?'

'He doesn't. But leave that to me. Are you certain Brigid, I mean really now?'

'I am. I've been sick most days mammy, and I haven't bled, and I just feel it. My body feels different too.'

'We'll go to the doctor to be sure.'
'I couldn't go to Dr O' Mahoney, I'd die!'
'We can go into the city. Leave that to me.'
'James' parents will be horrified. They'll be livid mammy.'
'Oh, they'll be fine. At least it's not their daughter!'

Brigid pulled away then, feeling stung. She stood up and walked back to the window.

'James' parents will be fine,' her mother said from the bed. 'As long as there's a wedding, they'll be fine.'

Brigid looked out the window and wondered if she too would misunderstand her child, like her mother had just done. Would there be a way that she'd know? If she said something to hurt her son, would she know instantly and get up from the bed and go to him and say she were sorry? Hug him and say, I'm sorry, I didn't mean it like that, come here to me now. Her mother hummed from the bed and when Brigid turned round Kathleen had her eyes shut and at her mouth was a small speck of a smile. For a second, Brigid wondered if her mother might be happy, as if Brigid herself would now learn about the world just like she had – all those dreams stripped away.

England came back to her mind as the sky outside was darkening and the ashy clouds were rolling over one another, as if in a hurry to a far-off place. Brigid stayed by the window with her hands joined; her thumbs slowly moved in circles around each other. Her mouth was dry and she licked her lips and slid her tongue around her teeth. A nauseous feeling started at her belly, something like a cramp and she wanted to sit down but didn't. A car passed. It belonged to Ciara's parents who lived up past the church in a three-story house. Brigid had heard Ciara boasting about the car, a Ford Escort that had the best cassette player ever. It was yellow and looked out of place driving against the stone wall, with all the greens of the fields blending so beautifully together. Brigid watched it drive around the bend and out of sight and imagined Ciara's parents driving through the village, taking a right at Church Hill, up along the road with all those gorgeous houses, into their drive that curved upwards, parking the yellow car, opening the door and looking out on the view before going inside to their daughter who has already finished her homework, and maybe has made tea for them.

Kathleen kept humming while Brigid pictured the grandness of their kitchen table, and the large windows looking out on the village and the fields that folded in on one another. She could see them sitting down drinking tea, with the teapot warmed in a lush sky-blue doily on the table, and maybe a plate of Custard Creams. The mother would speak first, very blasé, so Ciara, would you know Brigid Connolly that well now? Ciara would already know where the conversation was going but would answer just as blasé as the mother, not too well now, mammy, sure she's always with her boyfriend, so we don't speak much. Her mother would sit up a little straighter, and her left hand would rest on her right shoulder, that'd be James Maloney, wouldn't it? His parents are the salt of the earth, I see his mother at mass nearly every morning. I can't imagine what they must be going through. Ciara, with this openness now, would feel more comfortable. I know, mammy, and I always thought Brigid was so nice, so good. Ciara's father would clear his throat and say, it is shameful is what it is! And he would bless himself.

Brigid turned away from the window. England, she thought again. Fighting the word in her mind. It was not a country any longer but something else and it shifted, amorphous before her.

'I better be going down, there are potatoes that need peeling.' Kathleen said, standing up.

Brigid walked towards her mother.

'Come here to me, will you! Don't look so forlorn.'

Brigid put her arms around her mother's waist; her mother's arms were around her neck and she rubbed her nape softly. Kathleen pulled out of the hug and looked at Brigid.

'And be kind to James, you need each other every step of the way. And go lightly on him, he's a tractable young man.'

'Tractable?'

'Yes, tractable, Brigid, tractable. It means you won't have to be too harsh on him. He won't give you too much trouble.'

Brigid felt like laughing. She wondered if she actually knew him, really. Could he be using me all this time? she thought, dismissing it not because it was silly, but because it hurt just to think it.

'I know. Mammy, where are we going to live, how will we survive?'

'One step at a time now. Speak to James. Once you get yourself into a white dress quickly, I'm sure his parents will help out. They've money in abundance, all stashed away so you'd never even know. You'd swear they were Protestants.'

'Mammy!'

'Well,' Kathleen fought back a smile and turned away from Brigid and walked to the door, looking back only to tell her daughter to get ready for dinner and not to say a word about anything, that she'd talk to her father in private.

Brigid waited a little before going into the bathroom and splashing water on her face. She cupped some more water and put it to her mouth, rinsing it around her tongue and teeth before spitting it down the sink. She thought for a second she might get sick but the feeling passed. The mirror needed cleaning. It was her job to do the bathroom and last Sunday the mirror looked clean so she didn't bother taking the cloth to it, but now it looked back at her, stained and judging. She put her hands to her stomach. She wanted it to feel different but it didn't, just her breasts felt a little tighter, and her body in general felt heavier. She looked down and wondered what it would be like to see a large bump jutting out from her, feeling the movement of living inside. Her hands went under her pullover and t-shirt and were cold against the skin of her stomach. What was under the skin she could barely fathom. She tried to think nice thoughts or visualise nice things. But she could not and worried the baby inside would absorb all her worry and hate.

She looked in the mirror again, not at herself but beyond herself so everything went out of focus and even the bathroom became an almost blur. When she blinked, everything was back in place and clear, and her face was like it had always been but she didn't recognise it. When her features cleared and it was her again looking back, she had to put her hands on the sink as a wave of weariness broke over her.

She went back to her bedroom and lay on her bed, just for a few minutes, she thought, then, I'll get ready for dinner. She put Joe Dolan's new tape on and listened to *I Need You* and soon she was pretending it was James singing it to her. *My love's gonna last till the day that I die.*

Now

You wake up cold and try to pull the duvet back over you, but Ailish has snuck in again during the night and is asleep in the space where your legs curl. She is lying on the duvet and you want to tug it from under her. She has been sneaking in every night now. You and Nina are normally too tired when you feel her slide up between you. Her mouth is slightly open. She rises and falls to her own breath. How can it be so cold with the heating on and why will she not just stay under the blankets?

Nina is asleep. You reach over and take your phone and it lights up to show that it is only 6.06 a.m., and you have 48 unread WhatsApp messages. You try not to swipe across to read them, but your thumb has betrayed you and now sleep will not come back. Stupid GIFs and stickers, a chat in one group about the new online form to book a tennis court. People send their congratulations and praise. You crack your knuckles, put your phone back down and slowly slide from bed.

How can it be so cold in April? The raspy, carpeted floorboards moan under the weight of you. Yesterday's thermal leggings, shorts, thermal long-sleeved t-shirt, tracksuit pants and windbreaker hoodie lie on the ground. You put them on in the murky morning. It'll probably rain again but fuck it. You tie your laces and slither off down the stairs.

Outside is crisp and sudden. You get into your car and look back at the rented two-bedroom house and it looks derisive. You don't want to be there and it seems to know it, the lower windows smirk under the eaves. You drive to Crosshaven and park by the yacht club. The road is empty and the trees are droopy under the forgotten frost of dawn. You put in your headphones and step out a steady rhythm. You are angry at yourself as you start to up the pace. Thinking a mortgage would be easy, thinking things would fall into place so readily. Stupid, fucking stupid like, pretending again at being an adult, with your forced, ripened voice. Your nods and raised eyebrows; busy pretending to listen instead of actually listening. Thinking that by coming home you would in some way save her. All the thoughts come back to your mother and the entanglement of both your limitations.

It all seems calamitous now. You hear your mother's voice saying it, the way she used to. Softly, the slightest pause between syllables. Calamitous. But something about the move back, the certitude of something better, the believed cinch in everything falling back into place, now seems naively dangerous. The four-squared Tetris piece pixelating perfectly to blow two-line barriers away. Didn't you grow up there sure? Wouldn't it be easy, wasn't it home after all? You splash your way through puddles and find yourself running past your old secondary school. The big grey building is sturdy and solemn, overlooking the village. You feel all jittery and an encroaching upsurge of angst starts at your stomach. In that building is where you had the first bout of timorousness. Your mind used to drift in class. You'd look out the window and make up stories for every student that arrived late, or the cars driving down Camden Rd., or the nuns that walked from the school to the parish, or from the parish to the school, in clusters, talking to one another without lifting their heads. The lives unlived. Maths and French and Irish passed you by and when you think back to those days you remember the story you made up of Sister Margaret, whose parents forced her to have an abortion over in England and never told a soul, and then sent her to the convent where she took vows she thought she'd never be able to keep, yet in the years that passed she found solace in; a stillness in the silence. There was a language she spoke to God in that you imagined learning one day.

You're down by the pitch-and-putt course but your mind is still in the maelstrom of school. How easily the other boys stood up, stretched, swung their school bags over a shoulder, shoved each other, spoke, turned to have a look at the girls. How easy it was for them to exist. After speaking you'd feel physically sick. You'd sometimes have to go home from school early if you had to answer a question in class. Thinking everyone was just waiting for the class to end so they could mock the living shit out of you. You remember your stutter. Remember how unbalanced you felt.

You run harder. Some cars now on the road. You keep your eyes firmly on the ground that obscures beneath you. All those girls who'd smile at you indifferently, insignificantly, and at home your mum would ask about your friends. She'd say, I only ever see you with Fiona and Eoin, so you'd mention other names, saying you were all best friends. It only comes to you now, as you slow to a halt and stretch one leg against the curb, that she must have known all along they were not your friends. Of course she did.

Why did you not realise this sooner? You think of all the little lies you've woven and withheld from yourself, muddying them in the empty spaces of memory.

From nowhere, from everywhere, you miss your father. The enduring endlessness of his absence, of his non-being, memories only scattered of him, not complete, not real – you miss what you can't remember, miss what could have been. Your feet thrash against the ground, to the beat of all that uncertainty inside.

You run the way back to the car and turn up the music. Jeff Buckley plays in your earphones. You have all those running and workout playlists saved and yet now he lilts in your ears, *mama you've been on my mind*. His songs bring you back to your car. Inside, you pause the music, take your earphones out and everything is silent.

You release the handbrake and the complexity of how a handbrake works befuddles you. What happens when you pull it up, how does that simple movement stop the car from rolling backwards. More thoughts like this come back to you. Only yesterday, you were telling Ailish how the tide goes in and out each day and she asked how, and you told her about the moon, but you weren't actually sure. Then she asked, but how does the moon do that, and you had no idea so changed the subject. Now as you drive, you look at the windmills in the distance and wonder how on earth they can make energy. You pass a cyclist and wonder how the bike stays upright at all. You tie these absences of knowledge to the absence of your father. You think of all these little lessons that all fathers give all sons, all of them taken from you. You can see yourself, if your dad had lived a little longer, standing at his legs while he cracked the eggs, saying, dad, what even is an egg? And his voice up above you, ah, well, sit down there and I'll tell you. You picture his arms letting go of your waist as the bike moves to the rhythm of your legs. You also know that these spaces in your understanding of how the world works has nothing to do with your father and more about you, not wanting to find out the answers because they may take these images you can conjure up away with them. Outside your window the river is still and the last of the mist rises in silence.

You turn back at Whispering Pines. Enough, you think, of running. Away. You drive the car back into Crosshaven and up behind the church to your mother's house. It is still early. You go around the back, not looking at the small hill of the garden, and open the back door. You are quiet, worried your mother is still asleep. You walk into the kitchen and take the tea towel to dry your hair and hands and then walk to the sitting room where your mother is sitting in a pink nightie with a box on her lap. She doesn't even flinch.

'Mum, sorry for sneaking in.'

'Oh, darling. I was just thinking about you. Look, look here.'

You go and sit down next to her. She is holding old photos. You are just a boy in one, wearing loose denim jeans and a jumper with bears on it. You remember it, holding on to it for too long. In the photo, your mother is crouching next to you with her arm around you, and your father's arm reaches down and rests on the back of your head.

'Oh, I remember this day. I'd started back teaching and it was the summer holidays. You were so eager, do you remember, we were going up to Dublin for the weekend? There was some parade.'

'I remember the jumper.'

Your mother laughs. It is beautiful.

'That jumper! We probably still have it. James held onto it when you outgrew it. Don't ask me what the parade was but you were so happy. We all were. I was teaching again. We have such few moments really, through it all.'

'You were a great teacher.'

'I enjoyed it. Opening up imaginations. But when your father passed it was hard to concentrate. And I had you to think of.'

'I'm sorry.'

'Sorry? don't be silly. Only thing that mattered.'

She held the photo back up and examined it.

'Don't ask me what parade it was but you loved it. We all did. And I wasn't long back teaching. Was your father still working for Frank then?'

'No idea.'

'And the jumper, oh you loved that jumper. Your father used to say he'd always remember you as a boy in that jumper. He kept onto it, too. Probably in the house somewhere.'

'Would you like some tea, mum?'

'Yes please, drop of milk.'

You walk into the kitchen and try to remember your mum teaching, seeing her in the corridors of your primary school, embarrassed she'd say something to you. You remember her getting some award one year. You had to wear a tie. And your father was wearing a suit and was giddy. Swinging your mother around the sitting room. She wore a flowered dress and heels and you thought they were like something from a film.

You take the two mugs of tea into the sitting room and place them on the side table.

'What was the award you won, mum? One in the school, remember?'

'Me? Oh, the literary and literacy. Something from the government. I can't remember the name of it. I got it two years running.'

'I only remember one.'

The Language of Remembering

'I didn't go the second time. It was when your father passed.'

You want to keep talking to keep her. To ground her. You wonder how many other things about your mother you never knew, how many things you never asked her.

'Did you always want to be a teacher?'

The early morning passes. It is soft and pleasant. She tells you about how she wanted to be a university lecturer, tells you about the holidays she took with your father while you stayed with your grandparents, how they'd always go down west, how beautiful the coast is. Told you about when she was pregnant. How valiant she had to be. About your father almost going to England to play soccer, about his poems, about the letters she used to write him over the years whenever she couldn't put something to words. How she'd never send them. They're in the house somewhere, she says. The repetitions come and you do not mind them. You like hearing anything new, no matter how many times. She tells you about the fight they had with your father's parents. How hard that was. How she refused to stay in that house a second longer and how buying this was a dream come true. A house close to the sea, what more could anyone want. Then her answers slow and a tiredness comes over her.

'Rest there, mum. Will I get you anything? I better be going anyway.'

'I'm fine, I'm fine. This was nice, wasn't this nice?'

'It really was mum, it was lovely.'

Back home you boil the kettle for tea. How you missed Barry's. You take your phone out and scroll through Instagram. Then Facebook. Then Twitter. You call your mum. You want to thank her. You want to say sorry. Mary answers.

'It's just me,' you say.

'Oh, just missed you I think, Brigid was saying you were here.'

'I was yeah, she was in great form, how is she now?'

'Not bad now, would you like a word?'

'Go on so.' There is a long pause and you can hear your mum saying, no, no, in the background.

'She's not quite up for it now but she told me how lovely it was earlier.'

'No bothers. Call me if you need anything.'

'Ok, bye for now.'

You have the whole morning free and just a few meetings in the afternoon. 8a.m. Brazil time, 12p.m. your time. You like the time difference; it gives you the mornings with Ailish and Nina. You're not sure how long the consultancy work will continue, but for now it is easy money. With the exchange rate as bad as it is, it doesn't add up to much at the end of the month, but it is enough to get by.

You boil the kettle and pour some hot water into the French Press to heat it, swirl the water around and throw it down the sink. Take the ground coffee and scoop in large spoonfuls, pour the hot water in, and watch it thicken and darken. You want to have breakfast waiting for Nina. Sometimes you can see further down the line, things crumbling, peeling away. A distance doubling and doubling between you. Pushing the lid down, the smell of coffee reminds you of so many things: mornings as a child, walking sleepily into the sitting room where your parents were already awake with scones, butter and jam, and the smell of filtered coffee; the little coffee shop on the corner of Pedro Ivo, dark and gloomy, with the smells of beans being blended and the salty smell of pão de queijo.

You cut a bagel in half and toast it, Philadelphia it and put the plate on a tray with the French Press, a mug, and a little jug for milk. Upstairs Nina is awake and scrolling through her phone.

She lowers it and sees you tiptoe in. 'Oi amor,' she says, putting her phone away and sitting up against the pillows. Even in the milkiness of morning she is beautiful. Ailish is on your side of the bed. You put the tray down on the bedside locker and kiss Nina. She looks up at you and smiles.

'Where have you been?'

'Went for a run and then saw mum.'

Your stomach rumbles as you go over to your side of the bed to wake Ailish.

'How was she?'

'She was great. Like, really good. She was all chats, it was so nice.'

'That's great. See, there'll be good days, too. You just have to stick with it.'

'I know, I know.'

'Aren't you going to have any coffee?'

'Balls. I was going to have tea, I forgot.'

You slowly shake Ailish and she pushes you away at first before opening her eyes and closing them. Another little shake and she squirms into you and slowly wakes.

'I want my bottle,' she says, in the tiniest of voices.

'Ok, I'll bring it up,' and away down the stairs you go again and think of how the day will stumble out in little chores and tantrums and bargainings. It feels mundane, all of it, the world itself, a humongous ball spinning out prosaic plans to keep everyone busy, busy, running this way and that to stay alive and keep the ones you love alive, while most of the time never really living.

You pour the milk into the bottle and microwave it for twenty seconds. Back upstairs Ailish takes it from you and leans back against the pillows and lifts the bottle up so her face is hidden. Nina has eaten the bagel and is cradling the mug in two hands.

She smiles at you as you sit at the end of the bed.

'What?' you ask.

'I've a bit of good news but I don't want you getting all excited.'

'You better not be pregnant.'

'Why, would that be such a bad thing?'

'I was joking, come on now, what is it?'

'I have an interview on Wednesday.'

'What! Seriously? That's fucking great news. For what, I didn't know you'd even applied.'

'I didn't tell you because I know how your mind goes. Within minutes you'd have imagined me earning a fortune, and us getting a mortgage, and I didn't want to be the one to destroy the dream.'

You go to defend yourself but know she is right. Even in the moments since she's spoken a hopefulness has filled you up and your mind is already aching to daydream.

'I'm not that bad,' you say, 'but this is great. What's it for?'

'Oh, it sounds horrible. It's for a call centre, they always have such high turnover, but it's in Ringaskiddy, so I know that's close, and the salary is good.'

'Go on, how much?'

'60.'

'Fuck, can you imagine?'

'I can, but I won't and neither should you. I have no hope in getting it.'

'Why'd you say that? Look at your experience.'

'All of that is in Brazil. Besides, my English isn't good enough.'

'Ah come off it, will you. Your English is amazing. You're even getting a Cork twang.'

She smiles at that and leans over to put the mug on the bedside locker. She moves over in the bed a little. You move up and lie down next to her.

'You'll be amazing,' you say, and you totally believe it. Because she is and they'd be fucking lucky to have her.

'Finished daddy!' Ailish is crawling over Nina and reaching her bottle out to you.

'Wow, that was quick!'

'Yeah, it's 'cos I'm a big girl now.'

'That you are, come here.'

She finishes crawling over Nina and lies on top of you. She pushes her arms against your chest and leans on you with her elbows, and her hands play with your beard. You pretend to bite her fingers and she laughs.

'Daddy?'

'Yeah?'

'You know I love you this much,' and her arms stretch out as wide as they can, 'and this much and this much and this much and this much and this much.'

'Wow, that is a lot of love. Well, I love you to the moon and back.'

'I, I, I love you to moon and back and to Brazil and back.'

'Jeez, that is unbelievable.' You hug her and she lies between you and Nina and her little smiling head turns back and forth to look at you and then Nina.

'How about some eggs?' you say.

'Yeah, scrambled.'

You slide out of bed and make your way downstairs, feeling better already about all the little chores that await.

Then

The next few days passed slowly. At school, Brigid still held James' hand and they walked the corridors together, smiling when they were with their friends but not a word had been spoken of what had happened. Brigid hadn't told him how Kathleen had brought her to a doctor in the city. The doctor's eyes were speckled green and he spoke to her with no judgement and at the end she had an urge to put her arms around him and tell him all her secrets. He confirmed what she already knew and scheduled a scan in the hospital for the next month. All his words were soft, and his smile was crooked and perfect. She thought that he would never do what James had done, would never react in that way. As she walked with James now in the corridor, from French to Maths, she let her hand go limp in his.

'I've got to go to the toilet,' she said.

'Don't be late, you know what Mr Twomey is like.'

She walked away without answering and without looking back. She thought he was following her as she could hear footsteps behind her, all the way to the toilets. Only when she let the door swing closed and heard it open again did she turn and see Gwen.

'What is going on with you?' Gwen asked, walking towards Brigid with a sad old smile on her face.

'Nothing, 'tis grand.'

'Well, you don't seem grand. And James has been moping around the place, too. Are ye alright?'

'We had a fight, but it's grand I'd say.'

There was a low bench along the wall and they both sat on it.

'Over what?'

'It was over nothing really, the future. I don't know if we want the same thing.'

'Sure, we're only young. Don't be putting pressure on it now, just enjoy it. Jesus, what I'd do for a boyfriend. I haven't kissed anyone since Carl that time at Kate's party and sure he nearly choked me with his tongue.'

The two of them laughed and Brigid wondered what Gwen would say when she found out. She could imagine her asking, So, did you know then, that time in the toilets and you never told me!

'Come on,' Gwen said, pulling Brigid up by the arm, 'Mr T is already going to make a show of us.'

They walked back together and spoke of the homework they hadn't done, and Gwen spoke about how she fancied Paul, and they spoke about the weekend and for a minute or two Brigid forgot and it was lovely.

After school, she walked some of the way with James and she could see he wanted to speak but couldn't get himself to do it. As they reached the GAA pitch, where he'd turn up left and she'd continue on, he stopped and tried to take her hand, which she pulled away.

'Do your parents know?' he asked, not looking right at her.
'My mum does.'
'Right, right.'

She wanted to claw at him. Gouge at his eyes, but she started to walk away instead, rushing, hoping he'd follow and hoping he'd just bugger off once and for all. She turned back when she was up the road by the old three-story houses and saw him standing there. He could have been anybody. She walked the rest of the way home wondering what it was she knew about love at all.

Before she could open the front door, her mother opened it.

'Better you go upstairs, only come down when I tell you.'

The kitchen door was closed and she could see her da at the table, head in his hands. She wanted to go straight to him and throw herself before him and say she was sorry, cry her eyes out and say she was so, so sorry, that she never wanted to make him sad or let him down.

'Now, Brigid, for heaven's sake.'

Her mother grabbed her arm tightly and pushed her towards the stairs. Upstairs in her room, she lay with her ear to the floor, listening. She couldn't hear them properly, just loose words that squeezed through the floorboards and swelled, ripe and sinful in her ears. She thought she heard her mother crying. After an age she heard footsteps on the stairs and she shot up and went over and sat in the chair at her desk and opened one of her schoolbooks.

'He's taken it worse than I thought.' Her mother sat on her bed. Brigid didn't turn round and looked at the pen in her hand, trembling.

'Come here, Brigid, sit next to me.' Brigid got up and turned around and her mother's shoulders were slightly hunched and when she looked up, her eyes were sore looking. Brigid felt outside of herself then, splintered. She sat down on the bed; her hands wouldn't settle.

'I'm so sorry mammy, I really am.' Brigid hoped she'd say something, or reach out her hand but her mother made no movement and didn't say anything, so a sickly silence thickened in the air until Brigid couldn't handle it any longer.

'What did he say mammy?'

'He still can't quite get his head around it. He's upset Brigid, quite sombre. And, of course, there'll be all the talk and he's such disdain for all that. That'll hurt him, it really will.'

'Oh mammy, stop.'

'No, Brigid, I won't stop. This is not going to be easy. All of it from here on out will be intractable and you'll have to be strong, have to be ready.'

Brigid tried to say something but was afraid if she opened her mouth she'd start crying, which would only madden her mother.

'And another thing,' her mother said, now standing up and looking down on her, 'the quicker you both get to the church, the better it'll be. Especially for you, Brigid. It'll hopefully quieten the chatter at least. Now, get ready and come downstairs.'

Brigid felt weak. It was hard to stand up and even harder to open her bedroom door. Walking down the stairs was a battle. Opening the door to the kitchen took so much from her that by the time she sat at the table she was defeated. She was afraid to look at her da but the silence of them all, of the situation, was so opaque she thought they'd drown in it, so she looked up at him and his face was blotchy and he looked older than he did when she said goodbye to him that morning.

'I'm so sorry, da.'

He turned, only setting eyes on her for a second before looking away and talking very quickly in Irish.

'Don't! Just don't Brigid. You've no idea what to even be sorry for do you?' He stood up and shouted, clattering the chair to the ground. 'Do you even know what's going to happen? Have you thought about any of it for even a bloody second?'

He was by the sink now, pacing back and forth and the sheer volume from him filled up the whole of the room. Brigid cowered a little, her body leaning away from him.

'You think it's only about you? What about your mother and me, the life we built! Jesus Christ above Brigid, we'll be the talk of the village. And what'll you do? How will you raise a child? Have you thought about that?'

He didn't give her time to answer but went on shouting, only stopping to catch a breath, or slap his hands down on the counter. She'd never seen him like this and it scared her. He was speaking so quickly that she missed some of the words or didn't know them. In that moment he was so large and the sound out of him too loud. She wondered how it was the same man who had tucked her hair in behind her ear or lifted her up to bed when she fell asleep on the sofa, how gently he had put her into bed, before lifting the blankets up to her chin.

'I'll tell you another thing,' he went on, now at the head of the table, his hands on the wood, his head leaning towards her, 'you can bet all the money in the world James' parents will call you every name under the sun! Oh, he'll be grand so he will, they'll put this on you, I'm sure of it. Calling you every bloody name under the sun!'

The tears were already snaking down Brigid's face and she palmed them away quickly and looked down at her lap.

'I'm not going to be feeling sorry for you Brigid, I'm not! I can't even be looking at you!'

He turned then to Kathleen, who had been standing quietly by the door, just behind Brigid.

'I have to go out. I have to get some air,' he said.

"Ok, ok. I'll leave a plate out on the counter for you.'

He walked out of the kitchen without even looking at Brigid.

Kathleen walked over to the cupboard and pulled out a sack of spuds and poured them noisily into the sink.

'Get a bucket and help me here, will you?'

'I will mammy.'

She went out the back door and over to the shed and picked up a blue bucket and rinsed it out with the hose. The sink was full of dirty potatoes, and the water was running, and her mother's hands scrubbed them before putting them into a bucket.

'Let me do it altogether mammy. Your hands must be frozen.'

'It's ok, I'm not debilitated. Here.' She tossed a potato into Brigid's bucket and Brigid took a knife from the drawer and started peeling.

'Has James told his parents yet?'

'He's going to now.'

'I've heard that one before.'

'I know. But he is, he was going straight there to do it.'

'We might hear his mother lamenting from here.'

'Be nice, mammy.'

Brigid hacked away at the potatoes, feeling the lies tangling up inside her. She wanted nothing more than to tell her mother the truth but knew that she was on her own, now, in so many ways. She thought of what James was doing. What his parents would say. What if I have to go through it alone? she thought and felt the breath come out of her in sharp edges.

'Oh, just wait Brigid. Your father was right you know?' She threw a few more spuds into Brigid's bucket. 'James will still be a lad. He'll still play his soccer. Oh, there'll be little judging for James Maloney, but for you...you'll have to be strong Brigid. It'll make you into someone different, but if you're tough through it, if you're tenacious, if you can just rise above it, then once all this is done, the essence of who you are won't have changed.'

Brigid had stopped peeling but now that her mother had stopped talking, the knife curved again around the spud, stopping only to carve out the black craters and toss them with the peel. Brigid wanted her mother on her side. She needed one person. In her head, she imagined what it would be like if things were ok, if James came round and she didn't need to lie, didn't need to face things alone.

'What about the wedding, mammy. How will it be?'

'Well, I'll have to speak to the priest first and you know he's not too fond of me. Your father will have to speak to James' father to see about the logistics of it, money and that. The good thing is you're not showing, not really.'

'And will it be just us, just the families?'

'I wouldn't say so, no. I suppose your friends will go.' She said the word friends with an inflection and a pause.

'What does that mean?'

'It means, Brigid, that you'll soon find out who your friends are. Most of them will talk about you, the others won't want to be seen with you, and the rest of them will only pity you. You'll be covetous of the freedom they have.'

Brigid let another spud fall with a thud into the bucket. She looked at them, peeled, bare. All at odd angles, no longer smooth, no longer whole. Her hands were cold and pink.

'I'm not feeling well,' she said, and put the knife down next to the sink.

'How opportune!'

'Really, is it ok if I go upstairs?'

Her mother nodded without looking at her.

Brigid lay in her bed and thought of her friends. Sarah-Kate, Gwen, Bríd. What would they think? She had never told them she was having sex but always presumed they knew. She thought that surely Sarah-Kate and Anthony were at it. They had been together for ages and had no bothers kissing in public. She tried to think what she would do if one of them were to fall pregnant, would she distance herself? She could imagine what her da would say, probably something about their father or grandfather and how he wasn't surprised one bit. Her heart cracked at the edges then, thinking of her da, and knowing that soon enough all her friends' das would probably be talking about him.

She thought too of the soccer matches James would play. How she always stood in a huddle of girls for the whole match, unless it was lashing, but even then they enjoyed holding up the umbrellas and hearing the thwacking of the rain. She'd be the main attraction now. She could see all the other girls from the visiting team looking at her, sure they'd already have found out, more of them would probably come to have a gander. She didn't know what she'd do if she had to stand there alone. If none of the girls were at her side. But, she thought, I won't miss one match. Let them think me brazen, let the whole village think it.

She sat up then as there was the faintest knock on the front door. She ran out of her bedroom and was flying down the stairs to see her mother opening the door to James.

'Come in, James,' her mother said, 'were your parents rapturous with the news?'

'I'm not sure what that means, Kathleen.'

Brigid was at the bottom of the stairs and Kathleen closed the front door.

'It's fine mammy, we'll go into the sitting room if that's ok.'

Kathleen gave her a look that could have meant a hundred

different things and walked away, closing the kitchen door behind her. They walked in and sat on the sofa with the TV on, and Gay Byrne was introducing some woman she didn't know, dressed in a satin skirt and a cardigan that hung from her shoulders. The way she walked, the ease of it.

'What did you tell them, what did they say?'

'I couldn't do it, Bridge. I just couldn't find the words.'

'You didn't tell them. I knew it.'

'Please, Bridge, just let me explain.'

He reached for her, but she pushed his arm away. She looked back at the woman on the television. She was sitting on the sofa now, one arm thrown across it, her skirt rising slowly at the thigh. Gay said something and although Brigid couldn't hear the woman she could see her silent laugh. The suddenness of it. There was an abandonment to it, to the very way she leant against the sofa, and Brigid envied her every movement, every limb of her body.

Now

It's the end of May and the sun is finally out. You are driving to Fountainstown beach with your mum in the front, Nina and Ailish in the back. She was frazzled leaving the house and twice wanted to go back, once for oranges, the other time to make sure the door was locked, but now with the window slightly open and 96FM playing Oldies and Irish, she is humming and smiling, and turning her head and reaching round to squeeze Ailish's knee. By the time you park at the beach, she has called you all a collection of other people's names who she has loved and lost.

She links your arm and you walk along the low wall with Nina and Ailish ahead. The tide is on the way out and the stones give way to pebbles and they fade into the wet, muddy sand. Some people stop and talk to your mother, already with a tone of care and surprise. One woman, who you don't recognize, talks about school days and your father, she tells a quick story about a soccer match. Your mother smiles and the woman says, oh those were the days, weren't they? Your mother touches her softly on the shoulder as she leaves.

'The good old days,' your mother laughs a little, pulling you closer, 'she was a little bitch.'

'Mum!' you say, turning back to see how far the woman has walked.

'Cunning little bitch, I'm telling you. Talking about me whenever she could, pointing at me at the lovely soccer matches she remembers so well. The audacity of her.'

She looks content with herself and waves to someone sitting on the wall who squints and gives an unsure wave back. At the coffee truck, Nina orders coffees and a tea for your mother, a few croissants and a cookie for Ailish. You cross the road and sit at one of the tables. Nina is saying how lovely it is the sun is out, how beautiful the sound of the ocean. There's nothing better, your mother says, it could calm the darkest thoughts.

'You know, when James first got the car,' she's talking directly to Nina now, 'we used to come here at night. We'd put on our jackets and James would bring out a blanket from the boot and we'd sit on the wall in the darkness listening to the waves. The moon can do the most wonderful things with the water.'

'Was this before Oisín?'

'I shouldn't say this now, I suppose, but he'd be asleep in the back of the car.' She lets out a laugh, then Nina starts laughing, and then Ailish looks up at you all and she laughs too. The buzz of the energy lifts her up on the bench and she starts jumping up and down.

'Careful, careful,' your mother says and stands up slowly, walks around the table and takes Ailish's hand and sits her back down, squeezing in next to her and putting an arm around her.

'My beautiful cailín bán,' and she sways a little with Ailish tucked into her.

'What does that mean, Birdie?' Ailish asks and you jump in, a little too proud that you remember the meaning.

'It means pale girl.'

'Ah, will you come off it!' Your mother says, 'cailín is girl and bán is white, but I suppose in the expression it means purity or innocence. Comes from a sad story about a girl a long time ago, and there's a beautiful, touching song. Will I sing it for you, darling?'

Ailish nods and your mum starts singing softly, her voice an extension of the waves, a soft humming whisper that quietens the sounds of people walking by, the cars parking, the chatter from nearby tables, until she finishes, and Ailish hugs her tight. When everyone is finished eating, you pick up the empty cups and the napkins and walk to the bin on the other side of the road. Gary, a guy you play tennis with is also putting the remnants of his morning in the bin and you talk a little about the upcoming tournaments, if you'll play any, saying you have to schedule a game soon, and you walk away telling him you'll text.

You wait for cars to pass before crossing the road, looking at the table and seeing Nina waving to you, her other arm holding your mother up. You run across and start to hear the sounds of your mother crying.

'What's wrong? what happened?'

You put your arm around your mother's waist, lifting her a little from her stooping position. You try to guide her back to sit down but she is having none of it, she cries loudly and people look over.

'It's ok. It's ok, mum, it's ok. What happened? You're ok.'

Nina is at your other side, whispering – she was asking for your dad, I didn't know what to say, she thinks he just died now. I'm sorry, I must have said the wrong thing. You look at Nina and shake your head and tell her it wasn't her fault, that it's ok.

'Isn't it mum? everything is ok. Let's get you back to the car, will we? Come on, there you go.'

As you walk, her crying lessens. By the time you get to the car she has stopped but as you open the door she says, so that's it, he's never coming back? She looks up at you with the smallest, saddest eyes. You sit her in while Nina straps Ailish in. When inside, you turn back on the radio that is playing a song in Irish.

'I miss running,' she says.

'Running, you? I didn't know you ran.'

'I'd run all along the coast road, down by Myrtleville and back around.'

'Well, maybe we could walk it one day, what do you think?'

You start the car and drive away with the question left floating in the air, tinkled away out the window by a song you can't understand.

That night you go to Fiona's house for her birthday. It's an old Victorian style detached house in an estate up by Camden fort. It has the slightest of views of the sea. The ceilings are high and there's just so much space. There will be loads of people you haven't seen in years. You've seen Fio and Brian since moving back, and Stephen and Rose, and Eoin and Joanne. But ye haven't all been together yet, and you wonder what the dynamic of the group will be now, after so many years.

Katie is minding Ailish. She's Ailish's teacher in the crèche and you both think she's brilliant. When Nina first got offered the job, you thought she'd never like anyone enough to leave Ailish with. Then, when visiting Swan Grove Crèche, and speaking to the owner, Katie walked into the office, apologising for interrupting. There was something lovely about her and when the owner introduced her to you both and said she was one of the girls working in the room Ailish would be in, you saw Nina's face relax a little.

This must be Katie's fifth or sixth time going over to mind Ailish and it has given you a freedom back that you had in Brazil, where you could leave Ailish with Nina's parents whenever you wanted. Nina is looking out the window of the taxi and turns to you.

'Will there be loads of people I don't know?'

'There'll be a few alright but you already know the gang.'

'Rose is definitely going.'

'She is,' you say and reach your hand across to her, which she takes in hers and then looks back out the window. Herself and Rose clicked straight away and have been going on walks together and meeting for coffee. There are times you think she is genuinely happy here but the last week or two, ever since she accepted the job, there is something in her expression you cannot read. There's a shortness to her answers, to her patience.

'We'll have a great night. We can get horribly drunk and talk badly about everyone on the way home.'

She laughs but stays looking out the window. Without turning, she says, 'don't leave me on my own again.'

'I won't, I promise.'

She is still angry about the time ye were out in Cronin's. You don't know what happened really, you just seemed to move among the crowd, enjoying the conversations, enjoying the feeling of being known, so that throughout the night the drunker you got, the more you forgot you had a wife at all. It was like you were a different version of yourself, one that never moved away, one that belonged completely.

'Come here,' you say, and she turns round and moves a little closer.

'I'm sorry, I won't leave your side.'

'You can leave my side, I am able to talk to people on my own.'

'Ok, Jesus. What's wrong? what have I done?'

'Nothing, forget it. Let's just enjoy the night.'

This time you turn to face the window, knowing that it'll be hard, almost impossible, to enjoy the night if you both go in this mood. You hate when ye are not ok, and you can never fake that ye are ok. You feel everyone will know and will talk about it as they call one another tomorrow to go over the night's dramas. Oisín and Carolina were a bit off, didn't you think? I hope they're ok. Well, I know they're having a hard time. Sure they can't even get a mortgage.

The taxi pulls up outside the house and there are cars parked inside the driveway and down the street. You pay the taxi man and ask him if he could come back at around one. He takes your number, and you say, sound, thanks a mil. It's mild enough and you wait for Nina to walk round and she takes your hand and pulls you to her.

'Sorry,' she says. 'I'm just feeling a little weird lately. I like your idea. Let's get drunk and bitch about the world.'

'Chalk it!' You kiss her and she has a look on her face.

'What is it?' you ask. 'Come out with it.'

'I don't know. I just feel like I'm not doing anything well, you know? I was starting to enjoy just being at home with Ailish, taking care of her, even organising the house and stuff. I was just feeling good, like I was doing one thing really well.'

'I get it. I do. It's a big change. I think you're doing everything brilliantly if that counts for anything.'

'It does.' She takes your hand and then you both walk to the front door which is the lightest of blues.

Brian answers and he is wearing a Ralph Lauren shirt and

his hair is combed to the side. He is handsome but has put on weight. The house is lowly lit with candles. The kitchen has a large island and on it is a maroon table runner and there are little bowls of food, and rows of bottles of red wine. On the kitchen table are three ice buckets with Prosecco. In the corner, next to the oven, is a keg of Birra Moretti. You say hello to Eoin and chat about the French Open. He is the only other one of your friends who plays tennis. Brian comes over with a pint for you and a glass of Prosecco for Nina. She thanks him but you know she'd prefer a pint.

'Where's the birthday girl then?' you ask and look around the room.

'Oh, she'll be down in a minute.'

You know the others may think she wants to make an entrance, but you know Fio and can see her upstairs feeling insecure about what she's wearing, or the way she's tied her hair back. She'll be overthinking the whole night before it has even begun.

'Oisín!' You turn around to see where your name came from and a woman you don't recognise is walking towards you.

'Oisín, how the hell are ya?'

You remember her now. A girl you became friends with in sixth year. She had moved down from Galway and clung to you. You can't for the life of you remember her name.

'Hi, how are you? I haven't seen you in years. This is Carolina.'

'Hi, nice to meet you. God, you're gorgeous.'

'Nice to meet you,' Nina says and blushes a little.

She asks you about your life and you tell her. You try to bring Nina into the conversation but already she's drifted and when you look for her, she is sitting at the table talking to Rose. The woman, whose name you now remember is Rebecca, works in HR. As she talks, you realise how successful she is, not by what she's saying, but by the confidence in what she is saying. You then notice her clothes, the rings on her fingers. She is not beautiful but there is something attractive about her. She has very dark hazel eyes and dimples in her cheeks. Soon you are both talking about teachers from school and she remembers much more than you do. As she tells you stories, flashes come back to you. You do not notice her hand on your arm until you turn and see Nina by the door looking at you.

'So you were in Brazil. What was that like?'

'Different, like totally different. It's hard to explain.'

'I bet! And are you working here?'

'Not really. Well, I still work as a kind of consultant online for clients in Brazil but need to really find something here.'

'Sure take my number there, we can chat and I can see who to put you in touch with.'

'Ok, great. Thanks a mil!'

You take your phone out and swipe up and put her number in. You glance quickly to where Nina was but she is not there anymore. You go to say something but there are loud cheers, a few people clap and whistle. You turn and Fio is walking through the hall into the kitchen. She puts her hands out and swipes them down from her chest to her waist in a gesture to quieten everyone; her face blotches pink and reminds you of your mother when she'd get embarrassed. She catches your eye and gives you her awkward smile, as if to say, save me. You turn back to Rebecca and say it was good to see her and that you'd better find Nina. She hugs you and rubs her hand on your lower back.

You go into the sitting room, smiling at some people, stopping quickly to say hi to others. Your pint glass is empty, and Brian takes it from your hand and says, follow me ya bollix. You're back in the kitchen and there is music playing now, or maybe it was already playing and you didn't realise. Brian talks to you about the holiday they are planning to Portugal, saying you should join them.

'You can be our translator!' He laughs but you just smile and raise your eyebrows.

'It'd be great though, if ye could, like.'

'Trust me, you don't want a child on holiday with ye.'

'You'd be surprised,' he says and swallows. You feel like an idiot.

'We lost a baby, too, before Ailish.' You say and feel slightly nervous. You have never spoken to Brian about their miscarriage, only to Fio. You are not sure if he even knows you know.

'It's fucking horrible, isn't it? Fiona still isn't the same to be honest with you.'

'It takes longer than you think.'

He takes your glass from you and refills it.

'Talking of Nina,' you say, 'have you seen her?'

'In the sitting room last time I saw her.'

'Sound.'

You walk towards the sitting room and see a guy you half know and say, how's it going? and he lifts his pint up and says, living the dream boy, living the dream. In the sitting room, Nina is leaning against a side table talking to Leon, a guy you used to hate. He was friends with Eoin in school and as your group started to grow in fifth and sixth year, he became friends with all your friends but never with you. He was wealthy and tall and broad and good looking. You look at him now and he is very handsome. He holds himself the same way and kind of sways backwards and forwards while he talks to Nina. You remember him talking to you one day in school. You were both in early and it was just the two of you in the classroom and he stood like that, kind of looking down on you and every word that fell from his mouth was an awful cliché, like he'd been watching too much American TV. And he had a way of agreeing with you that made it seem like he was just pitying you.

'So,' he said that day, 'is Fiona seeing anyone?'

'No, not that I know of.'

'I think it's always so funny that people think you might be a couple.'

You remember the anger you felt then, and it rises up in you now as you see him laugh and fold his arms. You walk over and Nina turns to you and puts her arm around your waist.

'Leon was telling me about your school days.'

'Oh, was he now? Must be a very boring conversation.'

'How's it going Oisín? I didn't even know you were back.'

'Yep.'

'How's it been?'

'Grand, you know yourself.'

Nina's hand squeezes your side.

'Well,' he says, shaking his empty glass, 'I better get a top up. Was great to meet you, Nina.'

He walks away and you pull away from her arm and turn to face her.

'Nina?'

'What?'

'Why would he call you Nina? You always introduce yourself as Carolina.'

'Are you serious? I don't know, maybe I said Nina. Why were you being so rude?'

'I was just trying to balance it up a little.'

'What does that even mean?'

'Nothing, whatever.'

'Fine. I'm going to get a drink.'

'Grand.'

You walk with her because you don't want people to be talking. In the kitchen you both sit down at the table next to Joanne and Eoin. The music is louder and you can see it is hard for Nina to follow the thread of the conversation because of it. It used to happen to you all the time in loud bars in Brazil. You'd just be able to get words of conversations and would have to feed off the reactions of others.

'Do you know a girl called Lyndsey in there at all?' Eoin asks Nina.

'Sorry, what? I didn't understand.' You can see Nina cupping her ear with her hand.

'I was asking,' Eoin leans closer, 'if you know someone called Lyndsey Twomey? She works there in HR, too.'

'No, I don't. I've only just started though, so don't really know anyone yet.'

'Ah, it's a good company to work for. You'll like it. Lyndsey's a bit of a pain in the hole, though. So I'd avoid her at all costs.'

Nina laughs and looks down at her glass. Her hair is tied in a bun and from the side you can see how her eyelashes curl and flick up. The slight curve of her nose. Her full upper lip. You reach out your hand under the table and rub her leg and find her hand. She holds it but doesn't look at you.

You all continue to drink. You are already nearly drunk after what, four, no five, might even be six pints. Nina has stuck to Prosecco and helps herself from the buckets on the kitchen table. Rose and Stephen have joined the table, too. The girls are at the end of the table and you, Eoin and Stephen are huddled forward and laughing. Eoin is saying he shouldn't drink anymore.

'Ye know what I'm like after too many like, I'm a loose cunt.'

Stephen is laughing and getting up from the table and taking your glasses.

'Any news on a J.O.B?' Eoin asks you.

'Not a fucking thing.'

'Something will come up, you're a clever fucker after all.'

'Adulting fucking sucks. I mean, Jesus, when did everything get so complicated?'

'Don't talk to me. And kids, like I love Fynn, don't get me wrong, but sometimes...'

'You'd wanna throw them out the window.'

'Out the fucking window!'

You both laugh and Stephen sits back down with three pints. You clang the glasses together with beer slopping over and onto the table. You continue talking about kids, and work, and all the free time that you don't have. You want to ask something that would reach into the depths of them, something that would turn them inside out so that you could see that they are the same as you, that they think about the world like you do. You want to say, lads, I was an awful dick to Nina there 'cos I saw her talking to Leon, like why does that affect me? Why do I still feel so small?

And you nearly ask it but already know they will laugh it off, saying something superfluous before going back to talking about holidays, or shows they're watching on Netflix. You wonder, drinking back your pint, if they'd answer like that because they genuinely don't feel the way you do. The thought makes you feel inferior. Like you were born with the wrong parts, or parts from another life still inside of you. You look over at Nina and she is laughing, leaning over to pour more Prosecco. She is able to do that, to fight, and still enjoy herself. To compartmentalize. Whereas it is all a swoosh and swish for you – everything leaking into everything else. Memory and the present, or the holes of memory, the other lives you feel like living, the lives you imagine so intensely they feel real, all of it, like too many colours smudged together until they become a thick, horrible brown.

You get up to go to the toilet and in the corridor you bump into Rebecca. She is red in the face and laughing.

'Your wife is so gorgeous.'

'She is. Most people ask how on earth I was able to get her!'

'Well, that's stupid. You're a catch.'

You smile and she smiles back.

'I was thinking, we might meet for a coffee or something? I could use your help to be honest, to find a job.'

'Of course, sure you have my number.'

'I do, yeah.'

You hug her, then go to the toilet. While pissing, you wonder why you hugged her. Was it because she said you were a catch, or that she didn't seem surprised at all that you would end up with someone like Nina? Or something else you don't even want to think about. You flush the toilet and look in the mirror before going back out and talking drunken words to drunken acquaintances. During the rest of the night, you and Nina just seem to be at odds with each other. Everything she says you take the wrong way, everything you say comes out wrong. There is music playing and people start to dance. You want to but decide against it. You go and get another pint and when you turn to go back to find Nina, Leon is dancing close to Rebecca. He is stiff. It is as if his body does not belong to him; something between his brain and his limbs is broken. You go back to the group and smile at Rebecca and shout over the music, you'll have to teach him a few things! Then you laugh and move back to Nina. She takes your hand and pulls you away from the music and into the hall.

'You're very drunk!' She says in Portuguese.

'As are you.' You respond too quickly.

'I'm fine. Do you want to stay?'

'Of course, why?'

'You're just acting a little weird? You're coming across as a bit of a dick.'

'Me! Why, 'cos of Leon? You don't even know him.'

'No, exactly. I don't. Do you?'

'I knew him!'

'Very different things.' She walks into the toilet and closes the door. You walk back to the doorway of the kitchen and Rebecca and Leon are scoring, his arms around her lower waist. You see him pushing against her. You turn around and walk to the front door. Outside, a few people you barely know are smoking.

'I couldn't steal one, could I?' you ask to any of them.

Somebody gives you one and lights it for you and you say, sound. You walk past them to the front garden and look at the estate. All the perfectly mowed lawns. The BMWs, the Audis. You watch the smoke leave your mouth and plume into the dark sky. You think of all the other lives you could be living. If you were born elsewhere. Or even in the same place, the same moment, but your dad didn't die, or did die, but you were able to overcome it; the life you'd live if you never went to Brazil, if you never had a child; the life you'd live if you had studied for the Leaving Cert; the life you could have if only you knew who you were and what you wanted. You are annoying yourself. Your voice inside your head is screechy and irritating.

You flick the cigarette down the driveway and see the amber sparks scatter. Back inside, Nina is by the door of the kitchen.

'Have you been smoking?'

'Just one. I'll call the taxi.'

'Ok.'

'I'm sorry,' you say.

The Language of Remembering

'For what exactly?'

'I don't know, everything, maybe nothing.'

'Just call the taxi. I'm gonna head in.'

You take the phone from your pocket and you have 64 WhatsApp messages. You open the app quickly just to make sure none are from Katie. Then you call your man from the taxi rank and ask if he could pick ye up sooner.

'Well, I'm around that area there now, would ye be ready to leave right away?'

'Yeah, that'd be great.'

'Right so, see you there shortly.'

'Thanks a mil!'

You go in and give Nina the nod. She stands up and you can see she's going to start saying goodbye to everyone so you go over quickly and whisper in her ear.

'Better to just leave. Otherwise it'll take forever.'

You both walk out and into the corridor. Nina looks under the stairs where all the jackets are hanging in the wardrobe. You wonder if there is a specific name for that space, not a wardrobe, but ... there is a memory just out of reach with the word and your mother. You see her face flash before you. Nina hands over your jacket and you both walk into the night and stand at the front gate, your breath flinging out condensation, the two of you standing a short distance apart. You want to talk and just as she goes to say something the lights of the taxi pull up next to you and you open the door for her and then sit in. Fio and Brian's house gets smaller and smaller as you look out the window.

Then

'Is your da here?'

'He's out walking.'

His fingers moved up and down her fingers, softly, as if he was stroking the hand of an old, sick person. Brigid looked at the fireplace, the soot on the beige tiles that her parents had fought over. Her da saying how it was the most stupid colour ever for tiles for a fireplace. Her mammy saying how anything dark would make the place look morose, and how the house was sombre enough in winter. Brigid counted a row of tiles.

'I don't know what to say, Bridge.'

'Sorry, for a start.'

'I'm sorry. Obviously, I am.'

She turned and looked at him. His hands were in his lap now and he was bending his fingers back, pushing hard at the knuckles.

'Will you stop that, you'll only end up hurting yourself.'

He looked at her and she noticed his eyes were bloodshot and the skin by his cheekbones was pink and scratchy. She turned, lifting her legs onto the sofa to face him. He was still in the school uniform but the top buttons on his shirt were open. He looked very young to her, like a boy, really; a boy who for the first time realised the world was not made for him, that there were larger, moving entities more important and more powerful.

'I don't know what to say or what to do. Really, I feel like I can barely breathe, Bridge.'

She wanted to shout at him and say, you, you can barely breathe! Wanted to show him the idiocy of his words. But she also felt the need to cradle him, to make him feel safe.

'I know,' she said, moving closer to him. 'I know. Like the breath won't really go in at all.'

'Exactly.' He turned at last and looked at her. He had such a beautiful face. So clean and so soft. She waited for him to say more but nothing else came. His hands would not stop moving and his right foot tapped out quick bursts of tension on the wooden floor.

'I went to the doctor.'

'O' Mahoney?'

'No, a different doctor in the city.'

'The hippy?'

'He's not a hippy. He's actually really nice.'

James rolled his eyes and she wondered was he jealous. She hoped he was.

'And what did he say?'

'There's a scan scheduled for the fifteenth.'

'Jesus.'

He stood up and went to the window. She looked beyond him at what he might be looking at. The slope of the fields that not long from now would be scattered with tractors, harvesters, plows and harrows. And then the fields would turn different colours, a quilt-work of barley, maize, beet and potatoes. She knew he was no more thinking about what was to be planted and what would grow in the fields. There was something about the cyclical, about the certainty of growth each year that calmed her.

'I don't know what you want me to say,' Brigid said, not moving from the sofa, but pulling her legs in under each other so she sat as if ready to meditate. 'It's like you're blaming me for all this.'

'I'm not,' he said. He did not turn from the window but spoke to it so she could see his faint reflection looking back. 'I just really don't know what to do. I don't want to force anything but like, would it not just be easier...'

He didn't finish the phrase and she did not answer him. She let the silence of what he did not say fill the room. She wanted him to feel it, for it to descend on him, like darkness, or start at his feet like quicksand, wanted it to swallow him whole.

'Have you thought about it?' His head now looked down at his feet. She looked at his feet too hoping to see something else there but it was just his black shoes. One leg of the pants was stuck in his grey sock.

'I have. And I won't. I couldn't.'

'Ok,' he said, turning and sitting back on the sofa, 'fair enough.'

She had expected him to push it, to argue, to paint the sticky picture of their future. She was glad he didn't because she did not want to be convinced; afraid she could be.

'So, what's there to be done?' He looked at her. She wondered how he could be a father, with a boy's face on him still. There were sparse little patches of stubble on his chin but none on his cheeks. They were still soft and smooth and his eyes were big and his cheekbones cut high and she moved over on the sofa and put her arms around him, her head resting on his chest. She could feel the warmth of his skin through the open shirt. He was clammy. His heart beat a horrible rhythm. She pulled away and put her hand on his chest.

'I don't know,' she said. 'I'm as lost as you. Mammy says we need to get married and we need to do it quickly.'

'I can't believe this is happening.'

'Well, it is, James. It's our own fault.'

'I know, I know. I just can't believe it is all.'

'It's the quandary we're in.'

He shimmied a little away from her.

'I just think,' she said, her voice now a little higher, 'that we'll have to do what we have to do anyway, the sooner the better. Think about me for a second. Think of what everyone will say. Mammy says that at least if we are married there'll be less talk.'

'What, we get married in a week is it?'

'No! Obviously not, but soon, like in a few weeks. I don't know. But your parents need to know that's the plan. If not my da will go there himself. I know he will.'

She knew, of course, that her da wouldn't. That he could barely talk to James' parents as it was. James stood up again and now paced the room as if measuring the length of it with his strides.

'They'll freak out. I'm scared, Bridge. Like, you don't know how they can get.'

She stood up now, too, and walked towards him so they were standing in the middle of the room, face to face.

'Honestly, James, I don't care. I couldn't care less about what your parents think or say or do. I care about us. I'm terrified, James. Terrified. And I need you. We have to be together, really now. I can't be pretending anymore. It's killing me.'

She could feel her face burning up and her stomach lurched so violently that it left her insides unsettled. He hugged her, his arms around her shoulders and hers around his waist.

'Are you not happy, not even a little bit?' she asked into his neck. He didn't speak but squeezed her a little tighter, as if she'd know how to read the answer. The sitting room door opened and Kathleen's head appeared, then her body. She stood with her arms folded across her chest. James and Brigid unfolded from each other and faced Kathleen.

'Well James, you've got us all into quite the predicament.'

'Mammy!'

'Oh, sorry, did you get yourself pregnant?'

'I'm sorry,' James said, 'I really am.'

'A very small word,' Kathleen said, sitting down on the sofa now, 'for such a substantial wrongdoing.'

'I know,' James said, his hands rubbing at his thighs.

'And your lovely parents, are they as dismayed as ourselves?'

'His Da wasn't home,' Brigid said, standing a little in front of James. 'He's going to tell them tonight.'

'Is that right? Well, you better be on your way. Do send them our best.'

Brigid walked out ahead of James and heard him say sorry again as he walked past Kathleen. They walked out the front together and James kicked the wall lightly, sending the pebbles from the roughcast in different directions.

'God my heart, Bridge. Feels like it's going to explode.'

She put her hand on his chest and could feel it, battering away.

'I better go back in.'

'Ok, I'm sorry.'

'For what?'

'For everything.'

They hugged and she whispered in his ear that it would all be fine, that she loved him. Again, he squeezed her tighter but didn't say anything in response.

Now

You wake with your phone ringing. It takes some time to realise where you are. As you answer it, your head drums a steady rhythm; your tongue is stuck to your palate.

'Hello,' your voice is thick with last night.

'Hi, it's Mary.'

'Is everything ok? Is Mum ok?'

'We're at the hospital. She had a fall.'

'Fuck, is she ok?'

'She's ok, she's ok but she fractured her pelvis. And is very bruised.'

'Oh, ok, ok. Which hospital are you in?'

'C.U.H.'

'Ok, ok, I'm coming. I'll be there soon.'

You hang up as she is still talking and the drumming becomes more intense. You put your head in your hands and feel like puking. You go quickly to the bathroom and close the door. You kneel at the toilet bowl and cough but nothing comes. You are afraid to be alive. You try to place last night into a series of images that make sense. You cannot remember getting home. Did you fight? Should you say sorry? What if you said something horrible, what if Nina is thinking of leaving you, what would happen? Would she take Ailish back to Brazil?

You go to the sink and brush your teeth. You wash your hands and pat your face with water. Back in the bedroom, Nina is sitting up against the pillows.

'Is everything ok?' she asks, rubbing her eyes.

'Mum had a fall.'

'Oh no, is she ok?'

'She's after fracturing her pelvis.'

'Seriously? The poor thing.'

'I'm heading there now.'

'Of course.'

'Are we ok?'

'We're fine. We can talk about it later.'

'Ok. Sorry for being a dick last night.'

'We'll talk later. Let me know once you've seen her.'

'Ok.'

Nina sits in silence, scrolling through her phone while you get changed. You spray yourself with too much aftershave, hoping it will cover the smell of beer. You skip down the stairs, open the front door and it slams behind you. Shit, you think, please don't wake Ailish. You go to the car but don't have the keys. You have to knock on the front door for Nina to come down and open it for you. You say sorry, sorry, total idiot, sorry, grab the keys, go back to the car, start the engine and try to remember how to drive.

You are too hungover. Cars move in slow motion or in fast forward. There is no in-between. Your head is concrete mix. The

The Language of Remembering

fear is everywhere. You think of all the times you didn't visit. The more she started speaking Irish the less you started going. You think of the beach yesterday, how happy she seemed, and then, it all just shifts. You fear that. The shift. Never knowing when it can come. Afraid of the silence between you both, the length and breadth of it, the sheer weight of it. Afraid of the anger that is a little stone inside of you. You picture a peach eaten down to nothing. Grow the fuck up, you say out loud, as you drive too closely to the car in front of you. And will you ever hurry the fuck up, you langball, you shout at the car in front of you.

You park the car and walk the distance to the hospital. The lights inside are too bright and the smell of cleaning products turns your stomach. You go to the desk and give your mother's name. She is in a room on the fourth floor. You go up in the lift and regret it. On the second floor five people jam into the small space. You swallow hard many times until the fourth floor arrives and you leave, nudging your way through.

Your mother is propped up by pillows on the hospital bed. Her body looks painfully small underneath the white sheet. There are five other patients in the room, and nurses flit between beds, flipping charts and talking softly. Your mother's face is looking straight ahead and she turns it only slightly and she looks at you, but her face does not change. She looks down at herself and flattens the creases in the sheet with both her hands. You hover at her bed.

A nurse looks at you and comes over close, whispering.

'Are you James?'

'No, I'm Oisín. I'm her son.'

'Ah, ok, sorry. She has been saying that James was on his way.'

'James was my dad, he passed away a long time ago.'

'Oh, I'm sorry. Why don't you go over to her there and I can talk to you afterwards.'

'Ok, thanks.'

You walk over only because you can feel the nurse's eyes on you and you want to appear to be a son who is not afraid of what his mother is about to say.

'Mum. Hi, it's me.'

She reaches out her hand which you take in yours but she does not speak. When she turns her head to you, one side is swollen and bruised.

'Mum, what happened?'

'They're probably still talking about me now, and for what? Such insincerity, such callowness. Well, we didn't care, James and I. We didn't let it touch us.'

'Mum, Mary said you fell. Do you remember what happened?'

'Mary? You probably mean Sarah-Kate, Mary was her sister. Now she was brazen, that little Mary. What a mouth on her.'

You cannot think of more words. You look around the room and across from the bed is a vase of flowers on a table against the wall.

'See the flowers mum, what are they, lilies?'

'Flowers! Let them have flowers if it's what they want. Let them. It won't unsettle me if that's what they're thinking.'

She continues talking but it is all in Irish and the words sound violent. You stand up and walk away and look for the nurse who spoke to you. You cannot remember her face. If you heard her speak, you'd know it was her but no image of her comes to your mind. You tap the shoulder of a nurse who is hunched over a chart. She turns to you.

'Hi, I'm Brigid's son, Oisín.'

'I know. I was just talking to you.'

There's the voice.

The Language of Remembering

'Sorry, yes, um, my mum isn't making sense at all. Is that from the fall, or is she that much worse? I mean, she was ok yesterday, like not ok, but you know, not like this.'

'She's been more or less like that since she arrived. There's a doctor coming shortly, they're going to do some scans and talk to her properly. She was lucky it wasn't worse. The bruising will take a few days to go down. There'll be some medication she'll have to take for the pain. It was only a stable fracture to the pelvis, which means the bones are still in the right place, and only one of them was hurt, really. She'll still be in a lot of pain, though, and she'll be on blood thinners for a while just to reduce the risk of clots. She can rest for now but she'll have to start moving soon. Oh sorry, are you ok?'

You feel tears at your eyes and cheeks. You dab them quickly with your hand.

'Sorry, sorry. No, I'm fine.'

'The doctor will explain more to you.' Her hand is on your shoulder and it feels like she is holding you down, anchoring you to the floor. 'There are lots of support groups, too, for caregivers. I'll get some flyers and leave them by her bed. I spoke to the nurse who stays with her when she came in. It might be good to have a proper chat with her too, go through all the options. If you need anything I'm on until early evening so I'll be around.'

'Thank you. Thanks so much.'

She walks away and you call out, 'sorry, what's your name?'

'It's Noreen.'

'Thanks.'

You go back to your mother's bed and sit next to her. You take out your phone and text Nina. *Things not great. Will be here a while. Mum is completely out of it. She's breaking my heart.* Why are you always the first to cry? The room seems too small and your breath is stuck at your throat. You look again at your mother but she does not look at you. Her hands fidget, fingers picking at other fingers. You put your hand on her hands and feel them calm beneath yours.

'Mo pheata.'

'Mum!'

'An bhfuil d'athair ag teacht isteach?'

'Mum, I don't understand Irish, you know that. Athair, is that dad?'

'James,' she says, smiling.

You want to calm her or just keep her smiling, so you start talking.

'Remember when we went to Trabolgan, the time dad lost his shorts after going down the yellow slide? The look on his face, do you remember? And I couldn't stop laughing. I remember I was in between hysterics of laughter and being afraid, because I was laughing so much my head kept going under and I was kicking my legs as hard as I could to stay afloat.'

She is chuckling and takes one hand away from yours and rests it on her chest. You continue talking.

'He seemed to be everywhere at once, didn't he? The man couldn't sit still. Starting one thing only to stop to do something else. Used to drive you mad.'

'Oh, he was a divil for it. Unfinished projects all around the house. And I don't know how many books he started writing but never finished.'

'His poems you mean? Where are they now mum?'

'Books of them! Táid timpeall an tí áit éigin.'

'Mum, please, please just try to speak English, ok? I can't understand Irish, not a bloody word of it.'

She looks at you and her smile disappears so quickly you

worry she felt some pain somewhere. Then she looks back down at herself and hums so quietly you cannot make out the tune. You try to think of something else to say but nothing comes. You must have scared her. She's so small on the bed. You hear a familiar voice behind you and turn to see your grandmother. She holds a walking stick but doesn't use it as she walks towards you.

'Well, if it isn't my aloof grandson. How long is it you've been back now?'

You stand up and hug her. Her bones jut at strange angles.

'Sorry granny, it's been a bit mental since we arrived.'

'I should hope so. Keeping my great-granddaughter from me. I thought you would have visited me by now.'

'Well, you're here now. Maybe you can come back with me later?'

'That would be splendid. How is she?'

'A broken pelvis and some bruising.'

'Oh, I know that! How is she?'

'Not great. She's speaking more and more Irish. I can't understand a word.'

'That's your grandfather's fault, rest his soul, always chattering away as Gaeilge. Brigid, Brigid love, it's your mother. How are you feeling?'

Your gran sits in the chair you were sitting in before. You take a step back, unsure if you should be there or not. Your mother looks at her but doesn't speak.

'Bridge, how are you feeling? That's some unseemly bruising, does it hurt?'

Your mother doesn't answer but your grandmother doesn't miss a beat and gallops into a story.

'Well, the McCarthys on the other side of us have just got planning for an unsightly extension, and not just outwards, oh no, upwards too, bound to take some of our view of the hills, if only your father were around, he'd put a stop to it.'

You walk out of the ward and go down the stairs. You are still jittery. Your stomach feels full and empty and makes disapproving sounds. You walk outside the hospital and the cold dewy air is brilliant as you breathe it in deep. You put your hands on your knees and let the air out in little splutters. There is a bench nearby and you need to sit down but there is a man sitting there. You go over as your legs do not want to support you any longer. The man turns to look at you and you both smile at each other.

'There'll be rain, you can be sure of it.' He says, looking straight ahead.

You cannot answer but make movements with your head and your hands to show you heard.

'I'd love a cigarette,' he says, 'on days like today. But it's been over a year now I gave the bloody things up.'

You remember smoking last night. Flashes of Fiona's garden come to your mind. You remember getting the taxi home but nothing else.

'Are you a smoker?' he asks.

'Only when I'm after a few.'

'Lucky. Giving them up is painful. I nearly lost my mind. But I had to, made a promise.'

'Can't be easy.'

'My granddaughter's in there.' He says, jolting his head in direction of the sliding doors.

'Only eight, would you believe that? I promised her I'd give them up and that I did.'

'Well done, couldn't have been easy.'

'She's riddled with the cancer. I can barely stand it any longer. Her poor little body, you know? Tough to believe in God when you see your granddaughter like that, lost beneath the sheets.'

'I'm so sorry,' you say. He has put an image of Ailish in your mind and you cannot stomach her being sick, not even for a second. You think of your son and there is a pain inside of you that no words can describe.

'Will she be ok?' you ask.

'Oh, I don't think so. Her mother, my daughter, is stubborn, stubborn with love. The worst kind. She can't let her go but I think it would be for the best. It's only suffering now. It'd break anyone's heart.'

You feel tears at your eyes again. You want to put your head in your hands and cry. The day, the move, your mother, the stillbirth, it is all too big in your mind, your lungs, leaving no space to breathe.

'I'm so so sorry,' you say, 'I really am.'

He puts his hand on your shoulder and gives it a light squeeze and you remember sitting on the bench in the garden with your father. You try to hear his voice but nothing comes. There is a memory there you cannot grasp, or maybe many memories, too many to fix into one clear image.

The man stands up and says he hopes everything works out for you too and you thank him. You take out your phone and call Nina. The sound of Peppa Pig in the background.

'How's everything?' she asks.

'Not great to be fair. My gran is here, she might come back with me.'

'Will she stay the night?'

'I don't know. Maybe you can get Ailish's room ready, just in case. And Ailish can sleep with us.'

'Ok, of course. And your mum?'

'Not good. She's not making much sense. I'm gonna call Mary

to talk to her. And I'll speak to the doctors soon, but it might be time for a nursing home.'

Your voice cracks a little and you feel a stony sense of betrayal all over.

'It's ok. Go be with her and we can talk later. Eu te amo.'
'Também.'

You hang up and go inside and hover a little at the entrance. There is a board with lots of flyers stuck with pins. Lots of them for support groups, for room rentals, for missing people and dogs. One catches your eye. Evening Irish Classes. There is a black and white photo of books and writing on one side of it in English and on the other is Irish. You take a photo with your phone and walk back up the stairs.

Your mother and grandmother are laughing when you arrive. Your grandmother looks up at you and waves you to them. You look around for another seat and ask a nurse walking by if it's ok to take one that is against the wall and she says of course, of course. You drag it over and sit next to your grandmother.

'Oh my lovely boy,' your mother says and you smile.
'How are you mum?'
'Oh fine, a little sore.'
'We were just talking about your other grandmother, who, by the way, also wants to see you.' Your grandmother says.
'Oh, yeah? Do ye talk now?'
'Well, we live in the same village and most people we know are dead, so I have to talk to someone. Seeing as you never visit.' She laughs and your mother's face turns serious.
'You haven't visited?'
'Oh, it's fine Bridge. Give him some space. I know he loves me really.'
'Where's my granddaughter?' your mother says, pushing

herself up against the pillows and looking around, as if Ailish had been there all along, waiting to surprise her.

'She's at home Mum, but you'll see her now as soon as you're back home.'

'Is Da collecting you Mammy?' She turns to your grandmother.

'I hope not, Bridge. I've no intention in crossing over just yet.'

Your mother's eyebrows furl and then she looks at you and smiles.

'My lovely boy,' she says. 'I'm so glad you're home.'

'Me too Mum.'

'And Carolina, how's Carolina?'

'She's fine, settling in well now.'

'Ah, that's good.'

'Must be so different, a complete culture shock.' Your grandmother says.

The conversation flows like that for a while and it is delicious. It is exactly what you want. Yet you know, deep down, that these brief, incandescent moments are rare and will be rarer still, so you try to hold onto the words, the gestures, the lightness you feel as your mother swipes a hand in jest and laughs, turning her head and dabbing at the corner of her eyes. You want to sketch it so perfectly that it will serve you for months to come.

Then

Brigid sat on the wall outside her house. She was wearing a pink windbreaker with a floral pattern at the neck. The pockets were lime green. She looked down on herself. If anyone drove past, she thought, they'd think I was a little girl. She'd gotten sick that morning and when she made tea for her da, he had taken it back upstairs. Rusty, the older dog, sat next to her, his paw scratching at her leg for attention. She scratched behind his ear and his head inclined towards her; his back paw itched wildly at his belly.

She had called in sick to work even though her mother told her not to. She just wasn't able, to smile, to hold a tray, to concentrate on a pen in her hand, putting it to paper. A few days had passed since James had promised to tell his parents. Each morning at school she waited for him and he walked towards her, his hands buried in his pockets. She told him that if he didn't do it today, before lunch, her Da would be going round himself. It's an ultimatum, she had said, stealing the word from her mother's mouth.

Her hands were candy floss pink and her nose was running. She used her sleeve to wipe it, then wiped her sleeve on her jeans. December was coming, was making itself known already. It was her favourite month. The lights being put up in the village. The trip to the city to do her shopping. The break from school, just long enough to miss the routine and want to go back. The music on Christmas morning, the dinner that her mother and auntie cooked, the crispy potatoes, the thick gravy. The sense of promise and newness leading up to the end of the year. The thought that next year, I can be anyone, do anything.

The thought of it now made her catch her breath, hold it in and let it out slowly. People would start to know. The wedding would have to happen before Christmas, and even that, at a stretch, her mother had said, would be difficult. And James was dragging his stupid feet. They'd gone back to barely talking. His hand in hers felt clammy, it was as if she was holding the hand of someone she'd never met and it was awkward and clumsy. They hadn't kissed. When they should be getting closer they were being pushed further and further apart. She thought of when the fishermen tried to dock on a windy day. One with his hand outstretched to someone on the pier but the waves just pulling the boat further away. She wondered when she'd finally latch on again and be brought back to land.

'For heaven's sake, Brigid, what on earth are you up to?'

Brigid turned to see her mother leaning out from her bedroom window. Her hair was blowing and she tried to hold it back with one hand while pushing the window open with the other.

'I'll be in there in a minute.'

'Now! Jesus, preposterous behaviour.'

Brigid heard the window close on more words that never made it down to her. She rubbed her hands together and blew on them.

The Language of Remembering

'Come on, Rusty, round the back for you.'

Rusty followed her through the side gate and joined Rainbow, who jumped up on Brigid landing her paws on her stomach.

'Down, stupid dog!'

The two dogs stumbled over each other and back to the large shed. Brigid held the bottom of her stomach as she opened the back door. Her da was sitting at the table and did not look up from the newspaper.

'Trying to get sick out there, are ya?'

'No, of course not. I just needed some air.'

'Huh!'

She looked at the paper. There was more about the Ferenka workers, and the conversation around all the layoffs had brought a nice hiatus to the house. Hearing her parents speak about it, what would happen to them, the poor families, all muted the other conversations and Brigid felt bad for taking pleasure in others' pain. Her mother still going on about the queen and the silver jubilee and the potential visit, scoffing and saying, mark my words, next year will be abominable, a cruel year is what it will be if the likes of her are coming over completely unaware of the situation.

Brigid walked past him and went back upstairs. She spent the rest of the morning reorganising her wardrobe, stacking her books in neat little piles, and studying herself in the mirror. Then she lay on the bed and read over highlighted lines in her copy of Lord of the Flies. She thought of 'the beast', and the poor fighter pilot. She wondered how any child ever becomes an adult, how she would ever become a mother. It would be forced on her. She would not become it, rather it would become her. She imagined herself holding the 'conch', blowing into it, hearing it wail, feeling it swell. And then, when order was controlled, handing it over to somebody who knew what to do with it.

When the three little knocks came on the front door, Brigid was lying on the bed and wasn't sure if she was after falling asleep. She got up and rushed but heard the door opening.

'Tis yourself,' her da said.

'Hi Tommy.' James' voice was low and quivery.

'Brigid's upstairs.'

She was coming down the stairs and saw her da walking away from James, leaving him standing outside in the cold. The kitchen door closed as she reached the bottom step.

'Will I come in?'

'I'll get my jacket.'

She opened the door under the stairs and put on her pink windbreaker. She grabbed a thick, green wool hat, too, and shoved it into her pocket. When she got back to James, he was kicking his heels into the ground and punching a fist into an open palm. Brigid closed the door and they walked away from the house, taking a left, up to the fields instead of going back into the village. She was worried someone would see her and tell Belinda at the cafe.

They walked in silence. She was afraid to ask him anything. Worried of what he'd say if he had told his parents, worried what she would say if he hadn't. Brigid sat down on the curved, cobbled wall by the farmer's warehouse and James leant against the metal gate. It creaked, a high pitched sound that threw a shiver the whole way down Brigid's body.

'Well?' she said, looking up at the filthy clouds.

'They went ballistic. Mum slapped me and all. Dad told me I was a disgrace. And stupid. And all sorts.'

'Did they say anything about me?'

'Well...'

'Of course they did.'

'They were angry Bridge. They would have cursed anyone who came up in the conversation.'

'Did you ask them, did you tell them about getting married?' She wanted to say, did you tell them we want to get married, but knew it wasn't true.

'I did. They weren't big on the idea at the start. They had other things in mind. I was crying something awful Bridge. I think they saw then. After a while they saw.'

'So...'

'So, they said the sooner the better. They asked if anyone else knew. Asked if you were showing. I told them you weren't. Best be quick about it so, is what my dad said. I think he might be going round to yours later to talk to your da.'

'I feel sick.'

'I know. My mind is racing with it all.'

He was looking ahead and Brigid got up from the wall and walked to him, put her hand to his face and moved it so he was looking at her.

'What are you thinking?' she asked.

'Everything all at once. I was thinking of my granny, what she will say, and I was thinking of our friends, what they will say. Then I was thinking about the actual baby like, I mean, Jesus. I don't know. Where will we be? How will we be able to take care of it? What about school? Then there's the soccer.'

'The soccer? Seriously?'

'Well, yeah, like.'

He jumped down from the gate and walked past her over to the wall, so now she leant on the gate and he sat on the wall. He sat with his back to her, his legs hanging over the wall into the field.

'You know when I was up in Dublin a few weeks ago?'

'What? To visit your cousins?'

He swung one leg over the wall and turned his head so it was facing her, but he was looking at something above her right shoulder.

'Yeah. Well, I was staying with my cousins, but I was actually going for trials. There were some fellas from England over scouting for players and I'd been invited up.'

'What! James, you never told me. How couldn't you tell me this?'

'Well, I thought it'd come to nothing. No point in having all the village know only not to be selected.'

'I'm not all the village, James. I can't believe you didn't tell me.'

'I'm sorry. I just, I don't know. I didn't want to think about it. Then I thought it would cause all these questions for us that didn't need answering in the first place because I wasn't going to be selected.'

'And were you?'

'What?'

'Selected, James. Don't play dumb.'

'I was. And I was going to tell you but sure then everything else happened.'

'So that's why you were taking so long. If you want to go James, just go. Really, it's great. Just go then. I'm sure that's what your parents want anyway, so just go then.'

Brigid turned around and looked at the track that led into the farmer's land. There was a smell of cow shit and she looked along the track to try to find it.

'I don't want to go Bridge. Of course, I don't. Come on now.'

She heard him stand up and move closer to her.

'Bridge, come on. I wasn't hiding anything from you, I swear. I was going to tell you. Sure, I only found out I was selected the other week. It doesn't matter anyway.'

Brigid turned to him.

'Of course you want to go! Of course you do. Why wouldn't you? I hate this. I hate it so much. I'm scared, James. It's ruining everything. You'll hate staying here knowing you could have gone. I mean, I'll even hate it. Jesus, I swear I want to die. I don't want you to hate me for it. You'll end up hating me. I'd forgive you, you know. I would. If you wanted to go to England, if that's what you really wanted, I'd forgive you.'

He walked to her and she leant against him and he wrapped his arms tight around her.

'Sure all I'd be doing over there is thinking of you.'

She knew it wasn't true. She knew that he wanted to go. There was a lovely smell of clean off him, with a faint dose of deodorant. Her head lay in the nest of his neck and his arms rubbed her back. I'd go, she thought, if it were university, if it were something, somewhere where I could be myself all over again, I'd go.

'James,' she said, pulling away. 'Can we be honest with each other, though. Like really honest. I don't want you hiding what you're feeling. I mean, like this is it, isn't it?'

'I won't, I promise now. I won't.'

She took his hand in hers and it felt like it had before. Warm. And her hand fit snug into it.

'We better get back to yours. My dad could be going there now like.'

She went up on her tippy-toes and kissed his lips. They walked back the way they had come and he told her about the trials, about some Dublin langer who tried to sweep the legs from under him any time he had the ball. She told him she'd finished Lord of the Flies. He told her it was all a bit too mad for him, a bit silly like. She told him she loved it. As they approached her house, she thought again of the beast, how real it is on the island, how she herself could picture it perfectly and it was dangerous and brilliant.

Brigid walked in the front door quietly and could see her da through the glass of the kitchen door sitting at the table with James' dad, David, opposite him. Brigid and James hovered by the staircase. Kathleen opened the kitchen door and closed it quickly but not before they heard David's words escape. Stupid little shits, the both of them.

'James, go back home now. Brigid, go upstairs. And close your door.' Kathleen was already steering James out the front door with her hand on his back. She closed the door before Brigid could even say goodbye.

'Upstairs, I said!'

Brigid went up without looking back. She waited in her room with the non-words and grumbling from below getting louder. It's all she did lately, locked herself away trying to listen to decisions about her own future being made without her. Time dragged. She opened her copybooks and flitted through the pages without taking anything in. Every few minutes she'd realise she was holding her breath and when she let it out she tried to steal it back in quick gasping breaths. Her mouth was dry and she had to shove her tongue under her lips and push it round her mouth.

When she finally heard the kitchen door open, then the front door, then heard it close, she waited by her door to see if Kathleen would finally come up the stairs. She didn't. And when Brigid could take it no longer, she opened her door and crept down the stairs, avoiding the steps that creaked. She opened the kitchen door and her parents were sitting side by side at the table with their backs to her. Brigid walked around to the other side of the table and sat down.

'Was he alright?' She asked.

'Oh, he was only great. Over the moon,' her da said.

Brigid didn't say anything.

'The promising news is,' Kathleen started, 'that we are all in agreement about the wedding. James' mother will talk to the priest, the good Christian that she is.'

'The way he spoke to me,' her da said, talking to Kathleen and not to Brigid.

'I know. We knew he would though. Let him think what he wants.'

'And the way he looked around the kitchen. Did you see him? As if I don't remember him as a lad and what he got up to.'

'I know,' Kathleen said. 'I know.'

Brigid saw her ma's hand go under the table. Then her da's.

'It will be a very hectic few weeks, Brigid. It will be strenuous to say the least.'

'What will happen?'

'Well, starting from now you're getting married. So paint on an elated face and get a story straight with James.'

'Ok, ok. I'm sorry Da.'

'I'm sure you are. Aren't we all.'

He pushed his chair back and opened the back door and walked down the garden to the dogs and kneeled with them, stroking their heads.

'What did David say, mammy?'

'Oh, nothing we weren't prepared for. If I were you, I'd call round to James' house later. Put on that nice cream-coloured dress you have.'

'I'll be frozen.'

'Then put a coat on. Be pleasant. Apologise. And agree. Agree with whatever it is they say, even if you want to do the opposite.'

'Ok, I will. Thanks mammy. I hate it, you know. Making you and daddy feel like this.'

'I know. I know you do.'

Now

The July sun is just lovely. Your Nina is making coffee while Nina Simone's wispy voice oozes around the kitchen. *It makes me see what I want to see and be what I want to be.* Saturday mornings have their own routine now. You both wake only when Ailish does, which sometimes can be gone nine. Then you get up, take her from bed, flattening her bed hair. You let her watch your phone while you change her nappy. Then you bring her into your bed and she lies with Nina while you drive to the local Italian cafe and pick up croissants and cannoli.

Nina puts your coffee on the table and you smile at her as she sits down. This is the best of the weekend and you both know it. So far away from Monday. Now that you are both working, Sundays have become something else – hours of increasing anxiety. You sit at the table with Nina while Ailish watches Peppa or Paw Patrol or Baby Shark on repeat in the other room. You do not even dislike your job, but do not like it either. You take one sip of the coffee and open the notebook from your Irish classes and go over the words written on the page. Your mind drifts quickly back to that lunch with Rebecca, lunch that was only supposed to be coffee.

It was a few weeks after that night in Fio and Brian's, and after the hospital. In the midst of looking at nursing homes, visiting, pricing, trying to not feel sick at the patients, trying to not feel like you were killing her by putting her in one of those little rooms with a chair and a cushion that came off and acted as a pissing pot. Looking back, you were searching for something destructive. Something that would give reason to all the grubby thoughts, all the unkempt feelings that made you look at the world and your life with aridity. You met her in Carrigaline Court at 11 a.m. You were already sitting at a table by the window when she arrived. You saw her speaking to the waiter, the ease of her; then she saw you and pointed over, and touched the waiter on his shoulder and laughed a little as she walked towards you.

'Punctual, that's a good sign for someone wanting a job.' She laughed as you stood up and hugged her.

'Punctual or bored, I'll let you decide.'

'Ha! I didn't see you leave that night at Fiona's. Was everything ok?'

'Oh, grand yeah. You looked busy with Leon, didn't want to disturb.'

She smiled. The waiter arrived and you both ordered flat whites.

'So,' you said, looking at her, trying to act professional now, as if sitting with her were already an interview, 'how is life as a headhunter?'

'Ah, it's grand. Grand like. Hunter is a silly word. I spend my time scrounging through LinkedIn and making phone calls promising things I can't give.'

'Oh balls, not looking good for me then.'

She shrugs and laughs. The waiter leaves the coffees on the table and you both thank him.

'Tell me though,' she says, 'what exactly did you do and what would you like to do?'

'Honestly, I was a glorified translator. I worked for different companies, sitting in on meetings and translating. But then I started doing more. Like meeting with the clients when they arrived in the city, going out with them. Basically getting them to like me and in turn the company I represented. Normally there were lunches after the meetings, dinners, and all that.'

'Ok, great. And would you like to do something similar?'

'Em, not sure. Maybe not? Like, I've looked at jobs similar, mostly translation jobs to be fair, but they don't seem very mortgageable. That's the most important thing, to be able to get a mortgage.'

'And Carolina is working, yeah?'

'Yeah.'

'Do you mind if I ask how much she's on?'

'Just over 60.'

'Ok, that's great.'

She seems surprised and you feel like defending Nina, as if she needs defending. You understand why she gets the way she does now. How haven't you seen it before? The arched eyebrows of surprise when she says what she does; the condescending ooohhhhhhh, that sounds interesting, as if Nina is not meant for interesting work.

'And would you be looking for a similar pay scale?' she asks, finishing her coffee, wiping at her mouth with the back of her hand. You wonder if you've ever been in the presence of someone so at ease with themselves.

'Honestly, it would be great. But I don't expect that.'

'Would you like to work in a university?'

'Em, yeah, I suppose. But like I don't have a PhD or anything.'

'No, not as a professor. I know someone in UCC, they're looking for a project manager. It's to do with education and research with South America. Something about the administration and budget control of research networks, I can't remember. But it's a role of working with stakeholders and university leaders. It could be a good fit.'

'Yeah, that would be great. Like, not sure I'd be good but I'd do anything. I'm a quick learner.'

'I'll find out more about it and let you know. There'll be more, too. I'll have a look around this week. Do you speak Spanish, too?'

'Yeah, not really well, but I can speak it. And understand most of it.'

'Ok, that's good. Did you do anything for universities in Brazil?'

'Yeah, I worked for a good few events actually.'

'Good, good.'

The conversation went on like that for a while until you decided to have lunch and share a bottle of wine. Then you spoke about other things. And the less wine left in the bottle the more honest you were. Then you ordered another bottle. You text Nina saying you were going into town to check blackout curtains for Ailish's bedroom. She text back, ok, can you pick up milk and bread on your way back. Of course, you wrote, as the waiter arrived with the second bottle.

You didn't think you would do anything but knew that this was a betrayal in itself. Letting yourself get close enough to do it. At one point her leg rubbed against yours as she shifted on her seat and you quickly did the same, rubbing the inside of your leg on the outside of hers. Her face told you things you wanted to hear. You told yourself over and over you'd never do it, as if that made you a good person. You knew that what was preventing you wasn't a deep sense of morality, or anything good or pure, just the simple fact that you knew too many people around, it would be too risky. Though you didn't think that then, not really. As you picked up the glass you wondered how all the love you felt for Nina could disappear at that moment.

Rebecca went to the toilet and you couldn't stop your mind. You did not think of fucking her, though not because you didn't want to, but more because you have never had control on what you think and right then you were thinking about love and the brittleness of it. You knew you would never love anyone like Nina. Because loving Ailish was something altogether different and it should have its own word. You knew Rebecca was not as attractive as Nina, you knew the sex would not be as good, you knew that you would never love her. So why, you thought, wasn't love enough, there, then, to stop you?

Nina stands up now from the table and goes to the fridge and comes back to the table with apple juice.

'You not drinking that?' she asks.

You look at your coffee and the frothed milk has sagged, little holes showing the now tepid coffee below.

'Sorry, zoned out.'

'I saw that alright.'

You get up and put the mug in the microwave, avoiding the look you know is coming from Nina. When you sit back down, she reaches over and grabs your hand.

'Look at me,' she says. And you do though you don't want to. You smile and know that it must look fucking ridiculous on your face.

'What is going on with you?' she asks. You have no words but your fingers tickle the inside of her hand. She looks at you, waiting for an answer. Again, you make your face do things it doesn't want to do. You do not want to ruin your Saturday morning but you feel that your whole body is sick of itself, your thoughts are sick of themselves.

'What time is it?' you ask.

'It's nearly eleven,' she says, again taking your hand, canoodling it in both of hers.

'I love you so much,' you say.

'I know you do,' she says. She stands up and walks away abruptly, going to the back door and looking out. Her voice coming at you from her reflection.

'Whatever it is,' she says, 'I don't want to know. Not now. But one day I will want to know and you will have to tell me. Promise?'

'I promise,' you say. Your face is in your hands.

'It's just,' you say, 'my mum and the nursing home...'

'Stop,' she is walking towards you again and pulls both your arms so you stand up and have to look at her.

'I'm saying this so you don't have to lie to me. So there are no lies. And when I'm ready, I will ask you, and you will tell me, and we will deal with it. Tu está me entendendo, né?'

'Sim, estou.'

'Good,' she says and leans in and kisses you and then takes your heated mug and walks out of the room. You root around your pockets for the car keys, then scan the island, then the kitchen table before shouting to Nina to see if she knows where they are. 'On the kitchen table,' she shouts back. You turn around and they are there, magically.

'I'm just going to visit mum, be back in an hour.'

'Ok,' she says.

The nursing home is just outside Douglas, on the back roads. The fields are dotted with cows and there is the faint smell of shit and fertiliser. Inside the nursing home, the nurses are nice and friendly and say sweet things. They ask after Ailish and tell you that your grandmother is in there. When you walk into the room your mum is sitting in the chair with the blankets at her waist, your grandmother is at the window arranging flowers in a large floral vase.

'No Ailish?' Your grandmother asks.

'Nope, just me.'

'Pity. Oh, I didn't mean it like that. I just wanted to see my great granddaughter is all.'

Your mother's eyes are closed.

'Is she asleep?' you ask.

'Dozing. They said she didn't sleep much, disquieted all night.'

You walk over to her and her breasts are visible through her nightie. You lift the blanket up over her and take her hand. Her eyes open.

'Mo pheata.'

'Dia duit' you answer and her eyes flicker.

'James, ah James, bhíos sa tóir ort.'

'Mise atá ann, a mham, Oisín.'

Her hands start scratching at her arms and she turns her head away. You look at your own hands, as if they have hurt her. You wipe your dry lips with the back of your palm.

'Don't worry,' your grandmother says, taking you by the elbow and guiding you over to the bathroom door, 'she'll have days and she'll have days.'

'I thought learning Irish would help.' You swallow hard but whatever is stuck in your throat does not budge.

'And maybe it will! Now, stop looking so forlorn. You'd swear she was dead.'

She laughs a little and the sound seems to know it is not wanted. You think it before you can stop it. It would be easier if she was.

'I should go,' you say, turning away from your grandmother.

'Stay a little, let's sit.'

She links your arm and sits down with you on the bed.

'Brigid love, did you ever tell Oisín about the time you fought with the headmistress. What was her name?'

'Ms. Flynn!'

'No, no, that was when you were in school. I'm talking about when you were teaching. What was her name? Horrible looking woman, do you remember?'

'Wiry hairs coming out of her chin and cheeks,' your mother now turns to you both, 'should have been a nun!'

'Yes,' your grandmother laughs, 'oh, tremendously ugly, the poor thing. Tell Oisín. Oh it is a funny story.'

'I'd almost feel bad if she hadn't said all those things about James.'

'Don't mind that! Come on and tell us.'

Your mother brightens up and starts talking about your primary school and as she speaks other memories come back to you.

'Well, all that woman cared about were the academically gifted, and be damned with the rest of them. I mean, that poor boy, don't ask me his name, couldn't add two to three, but if you saw his drawings, and the paintings, and she'd give him such a hard time, and that freckled boy who'd dance when you weren't looking, oh, making art there in the classroom with his body alone...'

The Language of Remembering

'Yes, yes, that's lovely, but tell him about the fight!' your grandmother interjects, now standing.

'The headmistress, I can't think of her name, she had her own tea station in her office. Oh, she loved the thought of herself, and well, whenever she was unnecessarily mean to one of the students, I'd do something, like hide a mug, or plug the kettle out. Once I put all the teabags in the sugar jar and the sugar in the jar for the teabags. Well, she caught me at it. She thought I'd drivel and apologise.'

'Tell him what you called her, oh I got such a kick out of it.'

'I called her a warped, weird old woman who'd be better suited working in a funeral home.'

'She did! Oh, you came over that day, seething. Worried you'd lose your job.'

'I nearly did!'

You laugh a little with them and stand up next to your grandmother and whisper, I'd better be going. You lean down and give your mother a hug and kiss her cheek. You notice thin wiry hairs on her chin and remind yourself to tell the nurse to pluck them.

'I'll walk with you,' says your grandmother as she pushes her arm under yours and clings to it.

You walk the corridor arm in arm. Your grandmother greets people by name, nurses and patients alike. Asks an old, doubled-over man how his granddaughter's confirmation was, and he tries to bend his head to look up at her, telling her it was only lovely and wasn't the day kind to them. He calls her by her name.

'Jesus, you know everyone.'

'Well, I've been up here more than you.'

She does not say it as an insult but it hurts all the same.

'Why don't I come back with you? I'd only love to see Ailish, the little rogue.'

'Yeah, of course.'

You call Nina and speak to her in Portuguese. She sounds exasperated and you apologise but she hangs up without saying it's ok, or there's no need to apologise. In the car you feel stiff and heavy.

'So,' your grandmother says, opening her window a little so there is a thick bellowing of air that reverberates your eardrums, 'what is going on with you at all?'

'What do you mean?' You ask looking ahead.

'Well, firstly you're always so solemn. Like you're carrying something large and uncomfortable around with you. Then there are these abrupt visits. And the fact that when I reach out to you, you seldom return my call.'

'I've just been busy.'

'Busy! Busyness is not a just excuse, and if it really is the reason, then it's completely dissatisfying. Busy, we're all busy.'

She lets the silence sit in the car. She knows the powers of it and it unsettles you.

'I feel a little lost, if you must know.'

'Must? I want to know, Oisín. I want to help.'

'I know you do.'

'Lost how?'

You slow the car to the rhythm of the traffic on Carrs Hill. A light fuzz of rain falls and your wipers squeak. You close the windows.

'It's like, I've come here to take care of mum and I can't. I feel I'm making it worse. And life here is just harder than I thought it would be.' You want to say that you feel you don't belong. To Ireland. To your mother.

'Brigid isn't yours to take care of. That's not what you should be thinking at all, my poor boy. I'm still here, aren't I? And where is she?'

You wait as you think this is a rhetorical question and she will continue talking but she doesn't.

'Well, where is she?'

'In a nursing home.'

'Exactly. They take care of her. You can't do that. You have your own family. Comfort. Maybe you can comfort her, and even then it is only seldom. It's a vicious, heartless disease. Making shadows of my poor daughter. And she's still so young. Oh, she was well able was your mother.'

You look at your grandmother and she is looking out the window. Her body lifts to the breath inside of her. She is hunched a little, deep wrinkles set by her eyes and cheeks, and her neck is a wobble of too much skin.

Back in the rented house, Ailish runs and hugs your legs. You say give bisa a giant hug and she does and your grandmother smiles and says, something smells delightful, and follows you into the kitchen where Nina has her hair tied up loosely and is frying chicken. She turns, smiling, with arms out to hug your grandmother.

'Just have to run to the toilet,' you say, and leave the room and skip up the stairs. You go into your bedroom and sit on the bed. This is the last time you will think of Rebecca. You make the decision and you will stick to it. You feel the secret has its own heartbeat inside of you. There are moments you feel terrible, the guilt stacking and doubling inside of you, and then there are moments like this, that it makes you feel alive. That it is only yours. The only thing now that is yours and yours alone. A leaking of another life that has dampened this one. You think of the hotel room. You imagine yourself there again, but this time staying, this time lying back with her head on your chest and talking words that you cannot say to anyone else or in any other place but there, in that room. You play it out a little in your head and feel satisfied. You push the memory down, struggling with it like a ball into the water, holding it there and forcing it deep, dark down. As you walk out of your room you hear your grandmother's voice and you are starving.

Then

Everything was moving too quickly. Each day Brigid woke, she felt as if she hadn't slept, because when sleeping the day just continued in her dreams – the same worries, everything out of her control, the agitation at forgetting something and going to do it only to remember something else, the words not spoken, the tasks incomplete, a whirling of confusion and apprehension. She had never wanted something to be over so much. Just before falling asleep, she'd urge herself to think of the day with fondness – you're marrying the man you love, she'd say, over and over, like a mantra.

For a few nights in a row she had been having an eidetic dream of herself in a white dress, in a church she had never been in before, holding flowers, but they were all dead, with only a few petals clinging on, and James was so far away that she'd never reach him. Every step she took more people appeared, with their stretched, contoured faces. She could hear a heavy thudding sound and when she looked behind, her da was beating his fists over and over on a pew. Then she felt a sudden pang in her belly and woke.

It was always almost morning, so she'd lie there, worried, until it was time to get up. On the day of the wedding, she woke from the same dream and lay on her bed as she always did, and it was only when her mother came gushing through the door, rollers in her hair, carrying a dress from a hanger in her hand, that she realised today was the day. Kathleen hung the dress from the corner of the door and rushed back out without saying a word, without even looking at Brigid. She might have thought I was still sleeping, Brigid thought. She got out of bed and looked in the mirror that hung next to the wardrobe. She walked closer to it and stretched her face with the palms of her hand. Her tongue ran around her teeth. She swallowed and coughed a little and then went to the bathroom.

The wedding was to be at 2pm. In the local church. Her mother had gone with her two weeks before to a bridal shop in town. They had taken the bus. When they sat down Kathleen put her bag in between her legs. It was the largest handbag she owned and it was full and bulky. Brigid wanted to ask what was in there but before she could her mother was warning her not to have any notions. They were going to this shop because it sold second-hand dresses, and what was cheapest was best. Brigid told her that her friends had said there were places you could now rent dresses from, but her mother had said nonsense, that every woman has to own her wedding dress. Brigid had wanted to show her mother the irony of that statement by the fact they were buying a second-hand dress, but she knew her mother was in no mood for laughing.

When they arrived at the store, Brigid was confused, as on street level it was a hardware store. The window display was of tools, knives, sweeping brushes and large brown bottles. Kathleen rang a bell by a slim door next to the hardware store. Brigid hadn't even noticed it. A small, plump woman answered and they followed her up the stairs. She spoke to Kathleen as they were on the staircase and she had an accent from somewhere near Dublin. Brigid reminded herself to ask her mother after.

The room was small and on three of the walls were railings full of white dresses. Brigid felt the woman eying her up and down. Probably trying to guess her age. When Brigid looked at her, the woman's eyes were hovering at her belly. Brigid looked away and followed her mother to the first rail. Kathleen took each dress out and held it up and made a comment before putting it back – too grand, far too suggestive, I know we live in the sticks, but this is far too bucolic. Brigid had liked a few but didn't say a word. She felt as if this was all too shameful and if she spoke it would make her shameless.

Kathleen studied one for longer than the rest. It was a puffball and had ruffles and long sleeves.

'Try it on. I think this could be the one.'

Brigid took it and the woman led her to a small changing room that had a thin sheet to separate her from them. She didn't like the dress at all. Not that she had imagined herself in anything lush. Maybe it was the fact that she hadn't imagined herself in any specific dress that she disliked this one. She listened to the woman and her mother talking, firstly about the hurling, Cork's chances, then they started on a different subject before whispering. As she took off her clothes and put on the dress, she could just about make out her mother telling the woman that the fiancé would spend some time abroad, playing soccer, so they decided to marry before he went. She hadn't heard her mother lie about the reason before. Brigid wasn't upset because she could hear in her mother's voice that she was enjoying herself.

There was no mirror in the small changing room so she looked down at herself and noticed the dress fitted well. Very well. She didn't know if she liked how big it was at the hem, how it puffed out, but it was hard to tell without a mirror. She touched the fabric. It was rough on her hands and she noticed that the neckline had small beads and they moved beneath her fingers. They were calming. She rolled them back and forth with one hand while the other caressed the rich, rough fabric covering her torso.

'Have you sauntered off behind some hidden door? To a secret garden perhaps?' Her mother laughed and the woman chuckled.

'It's always the same,' the woman said, 'they take their time when they know it is the one.'

Brigid pulled back the sheet and walked back into the room, looking for a mirror.

'Oh, Brigid!'

She looked at her mother, who had her hand over her mouth, then both hands moved to her cheeks, then she folded them into a ball and brought them to her neck. Brigid moved to the other side of the room where there was a mirror. She took a quick intake of breath. It was like looking at someone else very similar to her, the sister she never had, and she wanted to tell her how beautiful she looked, how womanly. She moved her arms around to see how the dress moved with her. She swirled a little from one side, then to the other. When she looked at her own face it was smiling back at her.

'I'll have to take it up a little, I'd say. Do you know which shoes you are wearing?'

'I have them here,' Kathleen said, and Brigid turned round to see her mother take out a pair of white shoes from her handbag. They had a small heel on them and shined beneath the light.

Brigid walked over and the shoes had a pattern of little silver flakes that ran down one side of the shoe, and they glistened under the light.

'Something borrowed,' Kathleen said to Brigid before turning to the woman and saying, 'they were my own, believe it or not. Seems like forever ago now.'

The woman took them and led Brigid by the arm back over to the mirror. She knelt down and helped push Brigid's feet in.

'Yeah, thought so. I'll have to take it up, not by much now.'

The woman took pins from her pocket and started folding the bottom of the dress up and pushing little pins in various places.

'I could get it done for you today but it'd take a few hours, or you can come back another day.'

'Oh,' Kathleen said, moving over to them and putting her hand on Brigid's shoulder so she too became visible in the mirror.

'We'll collect it later today. We have a few things to do anyway.'

'Grand so.'

Brigid went back into the changing room and took the dress off reluctantly. She was singing in her head and remembered a summer in Salthill, down on the strand with her parents and grandparents, and the heat off the sun, and the slow, steady lulling waves, and the other kids jumping and diving into the sea, and a boat far off with a big, brilliant white mast.

As they went down the stairs and left the store, Kathleen said, we'll go to that nice café in the English Market. Brigid kept pace with her and side-stepped to avoid the people who marched towards them. Women with long amber coats and heels that clonked the pavement; men with caps and cigarettes, grouped together, laughing and looking at each other as they walked, not caring who was in front of them. Brigid had to focus on her feet, on the pavement, but her mind drifted. The magic of the dress had evaporated with every step. What if it's actually hideous? she thought. I only tried on one. What if the girls all laugh at the sight of me? What if James thinks I look like someone else? She could picture herself walking towards him and his face getting tighter, looking down at his shoes, coughing a little; she could hear light laughter from all around her.

'Oh, sorry about that.' A man said after colliding his shoulder with hers. She stumbled a little. Kathleen took her by the hand for a quick second and they walked side by side at a slower pace until they reached the cafe. Inside was all sound. It was impossible to snatch at singular words as all the conversations buzzed together like a swarm of bees. Kathleen nudged her towards a table, with her other hand pointing to it. They sat down and Brigid felt a little calmer. Under the table her hand rested on her stomach. The waitress came and Kathleen ordered a pot of tea and two scones.

'Well, I thought it looked striking on you. Have you thought about what to do with your hair? I suppose tied up would complement the dress and would age you a little.'

'Yeah, maybe.'

'What's wrong? I thought you loved it.'

'I do, I think. I don't know. I'm just nervous. Sometimes all these thoughts just crowd my head.'

'Well, that's perfectly normal for any woman before the big day, you're not unique. And, more so, neither is your situation.'

The waitress arrived with a tray carrying the tea and the scones. Brigid was worried as the waitress crouched that the teapot would fall and scald her. Kathleen poured the tea and broke her scone in two with her hands.

'I want it to be a special day, mammy. I want to look back on it and show my son photos and not be embarrassed, but half the time I'm just mortified and can't enjoy it at all.'

'A boy?' Kathleen's eyebrows arched making her whole face different.

'I think it is.'

'Well, I thought you were a boy, too. My mother thought I was, too. I think it was just wishful thinking. Look at me with three sisters, and your grandmother, there were seven of them and not a sight of a boy.'

Brigid smiled and waited for her mother to say something more but she didn't. Just as she thought the thread of her conversation was dead, for she'd never bring it back up again, her mother reached out across the table and took Brigid's hand in hers.

'It will be special. It will be special because you love James. I can see it, and he loves you. Everything else is...' and she took her hand away from Brigid's and waved it in the air as if conducting an orchestra, with her lips turned down. 'Now,' she said, 'I have some news. We've been talking to James' parents as you know. They're awfully dull, I don't know how they have such a charming, jovial son.'

'Be nice mammy.'

'Oh, this is me being nice,' and she laughed out loud and poured herself more tea.

'Well, as you know, you're marrying into a rather opulent family.'

Brigid frowned and stretched her cheeks. Kathleen rolled her forefinger and thumb round each other.

'Money, Brigid, they have money! Anyway, we have let them know that you and James and the baby are more than welcome to stay at our house for as long as you need.'

Brigid knew her mother was waiting for a reaction but in her mind that was always going to happen, it wasn't news.

'Thanks mammy,' she said, as an offering.

'Yes, yes. Well, the real news is that James' parents have finally decided to part with some of their gold and have agreed to build a house for you on the land they own. Now before you start getting excited, remember, they shall be your neighbours. I wouldn't wish that on anyone, not alone my daughter. But that is the situation.'

Brigid felt instant relief. She went to thank her mother but Kathleen was smiling at her own comment and nothing more, and when Brigid did go to speak, Kathleen interrupted.

'Drink up, we'll have to leave soon. I have some things to do before we go back for your dress.'

Brigid now had lost track of time while brushing her teeth and it was only the sound of her mother knocking on the bathroom door that brought her back to the moment.

'Hurry up in there, you're not the only one who has to get ready.'

Brigid opened the door and her mother looked her up and down.

'What a sight! Go downstairs and get something in you, then you can shower.'

Kathleen moved past her to the sink and Brigid walked down the stairs and into the kitchen. Tommy was at the table with a mug and a clean-shaven face.

'Morning,' she said, walking to the sink and filling a pot with water.

'Morning. Did you sleep well?'

'Not really.'

'Make sure you eat up, it'll be a long day.'

'I will. Do you want anything?'

'I've already eaten. There's bacon cooked in the pan there.'
'Thanks Da.'

He got up and walked to Brigid, who had her back to him. He put his hands on her shoulders and kissed the top of her head.

'You'll be alright,' he said and walked out of the room.

She cut some bread and pasted it with butter, put the cold bacon on top and ate it like that while slurping her tea. The rest of the morning gave her no time to think. She finished her breakfast, then showered and went to put on her dress only for her mother to laugh and say, not yet, Jesus Brigid, you've got to get your face and hair ready first, and with that Kathleen took the wedding dress with her and walked out of the room. There were knocks on the door and Sarah-Kate and Gwen came up the stairs holding their dresses over their shoulders and laughing. Brigid hadn't invited them, it must be Mammy's doing, she thought, but was happy for the company.

They got ready together and there were times that Brigid wanted to talk about the baby but she didn't want her parents hearing. She wasn't allowed to be proud or excited yet. She hoped that after today she'd be able to talk about it openly at the table, that she could tell her parents the names she'd been drawing in large, curvy letters in her mind.

'Where's the dress then?' Gwen spoke, sitting on Brigid's bed. 'I'm going mad to see it!'

'Ma took it, must be in her room. It's nothing special now. I liked it in the store but amn't too sure now.'

'I bet it's divine,' Sarah-Kate said, 'sure you could wear anything anyway and you'd be gorgeous.'

Brigid looked at the clock in her room and it was already half past midday. They'd have to be leaving soon. She was ferociously hungry. She walked out of her room and shouted down the stairs.

'Mammy, you wouldn't make me up a sandwich, would you?'

'What a time to be thinking about food!' Came the response from the kitchen. Brigid walked into her parents' room and saw the dress hanging in a plastic cover from the door of the wardrobe. She picked it up and folded it over her arm and brought it into her room.

'Oh, is that it?' Gwen asked, standing up from the bed.

'Open it up,' Sarah-Kate said, joining Gwen.

Brigid heard her mother on the stairs, and then the door creaking open.

'Sandwiches for her highness.'

Kathleen put the plate on the desk that was scattered with blusher, lipstick and hair clips, and then took the dress from Brigid and hung it up from the door frame.

'Eat those first and then you can put on the dress. Imagine, butter and crumbs all over it.'

Kathleen sat on the bed while the three of them ate sandwiches. Gwen said how tasty they were and Sarah-Kate said they were just delicious. Kathleen looked at the dress hanging, unaware of the girls' chatter.

'How I wish my mother had been there when I got married.'

The girls stopped talking and Brigid swallowed the food in her mouth. She looked at her mother and there was a thin glaze on her eyes.

'Are you ok Mammy?'

'Oh fine,' she said, shaking her head a little. 'Just lost in memory is all. Now, how about we get this dress on you.'

Gwen and Sarah-Kate made sounds of enthusiasm and Brigid took another bite of a sandwich before wiping her hands on a towel and taking the dress in her arms. She didn't want to undress in front of her friends, now acutely aware of the slight bulge at her belly.

'Mammy, will you come with me in the bathroom?'

Kathleen didn't answer but stood up and walked with her.

Brigid took off her clothes with her back to her mother. She unclipped her bra, both hands fiddling with the clasp behind her back. Kathleen took the dress from the plastic and held it up straight with both arms, admiring it or questioning it, Brigid couldn't tell. Brigid held onto the wall as she lifted one leg over, using her other hand to shuffle into the bottom of the dress until her foot touched the floor. Then put the other leg in. Her mother lifted it, shimmying it until Brigid's breasts were against the fabric. She turned around and Kathleen zipped up the first part of the dress to her waist, and then fastened the buttons, forcing Brigid to breathe in tight. She turned to face her mother. Kathleen was smiling; it stuck between her cheeks as she tried not to cry.

'My little girl,' was all she said before kissing her lightly on the cheek and making her way back downstairs.

Now

You slide chopped carrots, onions, garlic, rosemary and thyme into melted butter in the wok and listen to the hiss as you breathe in the smell of your mother's cooking. Cohen half sings, half speaks to you, *a million candles burning for the help that never came*. You imagine the church where you did your first communion, how your mother gave you some spare change to go and light thin, waxy candles that had already been lit and blown out. You were meant to light them for your grandfathers but instead made wishes that never came true.

As you stir in the minced meat, Cohen sings that *there's a lullaby for suffering, and a paradox to blame*, and you agree, know this is true, but cannot label this truth to anything that makes sense. You add tomato puree, a tablespoon of flour, and stir. Ailish is at your legs. Daddy need help? Not now and be careful, the oven is on and is very, very hot. Too hot, she asks. Yes, too hot.

You've been speaking more and more English to Ailish

lately. You worry about her Portuguese, about her tie to her grandparents, her aunties and cousins, to Brazil. You haven't called Nina today and know she will be waiting. Stuck up in Dublin for a few days of meetings, a city she dislikes for its greyness, and the accents she still cannot understand. She has been up to Dublin most weeks and never just for the day. You have had to calm your mind from the war it rages. She hates being needy and will be waiting for you to call so she can vent about being fed up with her colleagues, with the traffic, with the cold. You will stop yourself from asking boyish questions. You will call her on the way to class.

You turn off the hob and add freshly chopped parsley. Pour it from the wok into a large, glass oval serving dish. Take the mashed potatoes with aged cheddar cheese and dollop it on top of the meat mixture. Your mother's arms were constantly burnt and scarred from leaning across naked flames or reaching into the darkness of the oven. She never listened to music or the radio but hummed songs her mother used to sing to her.

When she did sing, the lyrics were always as Gaeilge so you would only understand a few words, croí, bás, brón. You remember when you were very young, and your grandfather was alive, the language made sense to you. You'd listen as they all spoke around the fire with large mugs of tea. It was like listening to music, the words were all known, but put together in adult talk they became obscure or inscrutable.

You open a bottle of wine and pour a glass. From the kitchen counter you lean around the door into the sitting room and Ailish is talking a mix of words and sounds with a doll in either hand, and the sight of her, leaning forward on her knees, living another world inside her head, makes you feel warm and yet you fight the urge to cry. It is so easy for her to communicate, with you, with the doll, with the very air around her, which she talks to when it is too cold or too hot. The sounds she can make, the notes and tones that are not quite words but contain all the meaning in the world. You understand her sighs, the sticky thud she makes with her tongue on her palate when excited. There is no language needed, no syntax, no agreements.

In the second or third class is when the words stopped making sense to you. The Irish language became shapes and noises, and, even for a time, English became a fuzz of black and white. You stopped reading. You stopped being able to write your name. You remember your mother on the phone downstairs calling friends, relatives, repeating questions, scraping pleas from the back of her throat. She didn't have the money for the doctors needed, the ones whose names she whispered; now with her husband in the ground, she didn't have the time.

You remember your granny pacing in the kitchen. You were playing games in the sitting room but the door was open and you pretended not to be listening.

'Oh, for heaven's sake Brigid, just ask them, don't be so adamant, especially when you're wrong.'

'I won't mammy, I won't. Not after what they said, I mean after all these years!'

She brought you once to a centre where the waiting stretched out like the rows of plastic chairs. When your name was called, a tall woman with very large glasses asked your mother to wait and you went with the woman into a room where there was a sofa and lots of toys to play with. She spoke some words in Irish to you, they sounded like grass being cut. Then she asked you your age in English and what you liked to do. You reached into one of the boxes and pulled out a plastic telephone that had the ring of numbers and you put your finger to the hole of number four and pulled it round and listened to it click click click all the way back into its place. It was your favourite number; your father's favourite number. You wondered what happened to numbers that wanted to be words.

She asked about your father and you told her how your mother came into your room to tell you he had gone and how you thought of how the word 'go' still had an association with 'where', 'place', 'return.' She told you that your mother told her it was you who had been with him, sitting out in the garden. When he fell from the bench, clutching at his chest, his eyes open looking up at the ballooning grey clouds. It was you who were with him. Maybe, you said, could be. I don't remember. She told you it had been a short time ago, and you said yes, maybe, could be. But it feels like so much longer.

Later she opened a book and asked if you liked it. You nodded and looked up from where you were sitting into her eyes, which were magnified by her glasses so she looked cartoonish. Why don't you read it to me? The words were beautiful shapes that scattered down the page like black rainfall. There was a design in the white spaces. You imagined a tiny little ball falling in between the cracks trying to get to the end. You squinted and the words looked like tiny birds flying against clouds. You closed the book and handed it back to her and walked out of the room without being able to say, thank you, or goodbye, or sorry. You felt the need to apologise but for what you weren't exactly sure.

You take the glass of wine and sit on the sofa in the sitting room and Ailish climbs up next to you and puts her arms around one of your arms and her head on your shoulder and clicks her tongue. If this is not language then you don't know what is. She leaves the room quickly and you hear her feet on the stairs. She has gone up them and down them a million times yet every time

The Language of Remembering

you still see her fallen at the bottom of the stairs, head twisted to the wrong side, eyes agape, blood at her mouth. Her legs shuffle against each other as she comes back in with The Gruffalo and sits back down and opens it up. You read it and she reads along even though the letters don't make sense to her yet – she has it all in her head, a pre-language of sorts.

Your mobile rings. While finding it you think of how the mouse fools them all, and you wonder if you can fool your own mind into remembering your dad, the bench. The nurse talks in hurried, breathy phrases. In the nursing home they speak like this. You know they must have a list of similar calls to make. Suddenly you miss Mary, wonder why you never sent her a hamper like you said you would. You talk back. Yes. Tomorrow, ok. Lunchtime. No, just me. Then you hang up and walk into the kitchen and look into the oven without checking to see if the potatoes are browning and the cheddar is melting and starting to crisp. You hope it will be ready before you have to leave for your class. You try to remember the word for daughter, for mother, for hope.

The Gruffalo is on the floor and your daughter runs to your legs again, holds you and says, I love you too much. You say, my girl, my girl. She looks up and smiles the most perfect little teeth and says, my daddy, my daddy. You know there is nothing more beautiful that language can offer. You sit on the sofa with her and tell her you have to go out tonight but Katie will babysit and you won't be long. She doesn't say anything but licks her lips and fiddles her thumbs together and curls her fingers as if stretching something between them, casting an answer in the air. I know, you say, but I have to, I won't be long.

You take the Cottage Pie from the oven and let it cool on the counter. You will eat when you get back. When Katie arrives your daughter sulks but you turn on the TV for her and say she can watch two full episodes of Paw Patrol before dinner. She half smiles and blows you a kiss as you walk out the front door. In the car you practice words in your head, little phrases. You wonder what good it will do, knowing how to say it is sunny, or that you are hungry, or that you are thirty-five years-old, when what you really want to say is too convoluted for any language.

You are one of the first to arrive and the seats are in a circle and there is a ball in the middle and the teacher, Seán, walks to meet you and puts out his hand and says, conas atá tú inniu, Oisín? You smile and feel awkward and say táim ceart go leor, táim ceart go leor. Even though you are not, even though the word for what you are is cemented somewhere inside of you. You imagine whatever it is being pulled out and you hear it clatter into a metal, surgical tray, echoing.

As you sit down you remember getting your deviated septum fixed, how on the first visit to the doctor after the surgery, he lay you back on his chair and shoved the cotton on the end of the forceps into each nostril, pushing them inwards and upwards until you felt them by your eye sockets. Then he cut at hardened things inside your nostrils and used the forceps again to pull the soggy, crimson cotton free. It was such an invasion you thought you'd pass out. Then afterwards he asked you to breathe through your nose and you felt clogs of blood squirm down the back of your throat. Then there was so much air. You would like to be able to breathe like that again.

The game begins when the rest of the students arrive. The objective is to say three things about yourself, two of them are true and one of them is false. Then you throw the ball to someone and they have to guess which one is false. You are nervous because you cannot think of what to say and really want to use these classes to find the words you have to say, but it is week seven and still you haven't said máthair, cuimhne, bás.

There is a woman with a pointy face who starts, you cannot say what exactly it is that makes it pointy because when you focus on her nose or her chin, they do not look overly pronged, but the umbrella of all of her features makes her look indignant and aciculate. She throws the ball to you and you can only understand one of the things she said, which is she lived abroad for a year, and even though you think it's true you say it's false, but can't remember the word for false so just say it in English, and then she answers no, that it is not bréagach, and that she actually lived in France and speaks four languages. What was false about her was that she had once owned a bakery. You didn't know the word for that, bácús.

It is your turn and your heart thickens. The sensation reminds you of being a teenager, afraid your voice would break while having to read Heaney's *Digging* aloud in assembly one morning. It had been a punishment for something and you had read the poem a hundred times before having to stand up and read it aloud, and each time you read it you thought of your father, his pen scrawling letters in leather bound notebooks. You wonder where they could be now and think of asking your mother again, and even though you know the word for notebook you do not know if you could put it in a question. Anois, bain triail as, Seán says and smiles at you. Well, you say. Well, you say again and for the life of you, you cannot think of any truth you feel like sharing. The only lie that comes to you is that your father is still alive but that doesn't seem appropriate. Sometimes it feels like a truth. You think he is alive somewhere for his death is a memory that is not complete and therefore not completely real. At so many moments through your life you have imagined him just too far away, and when you, on the rare occasion say, I wish my dad could be here, in your head you imagine him alive, elsewhere, wishing too that he could be there. Tá iníon amháin agam, you say and picture your daughter's face, probably getting impatient already, refusing to go to bed without you. You have one daughter, which is the truth, but seems like a lie. You think of the stillbirth, your baby boy, who had the name of your father.

They all look at you, waiting for the next truth or lie but your mind will not sit still. You try to stop yourself but start looking at each of them, making shot-fire stories up in your head. The large man who wears a vested jacket is a farmer, his brothers are at familiar war over the land and speak about him in Irish in the darkness of night. That kind, teapot-looking lady is a recent widow who finds ways to forget. The guy who is around the same age as you, who can grow a full, feathery beard needs Irish for a government job, one he will spend years at until finally he is able to retire. He will look back on the days like ripples that never rippled. You stand up and kind of smile. You cough a little and go to say something but nothing comes. You feel language float away. It is like letting go of a kite – it is not the weight that you cannot feel but the sense of holding on.

The sound in the room has vacuumed elsewhere and you see Seán's mouth move in moon shapes. They all look like memories or remembering a dream from years ago. You feel like this has happened before, countless times, and you are just reliving it, moving your body from beneath string. You feel your left foot take a step backwards and with that your body turns. You are leaving the room until you realise you are still holding the ball, so you turn back around, bend down and roll it gently back into the circle.

Back in the car you call your wife and imagine her sitting by the window of her hotel room looking out on the shitty weather,

The Language of Remembering

feeling shitty herself. She answers and says in Portuguese, aren't you supposed to be in that evening class, and you say yes, but you left. Why, she asks, and you sigh and if a sigh could echo in a car it would but it can't so it doesn't. How's your mum? she asks. I'll see her tomorrow. Are you bringing Ailish? No, Katie will mind her. You should bring her, she says, it might cheer your mum up, who knows it might get her speaking English.

You sigh again because you no longer miss your mum but who your mum was – the way she turned a phrase and how it hung in the air long after it was spoken; how she could see everything from an angle inexistent to the naked eye; you miss the way she looked at you. Every time you see her now, you miss her knowing who you are all of the time. Miss being able to understand her.

'Well,' you say, 'I better get back home.'

'Ok.'

'Wait,' you say. 'Do you ever think about him?'

'About who?'

'Our son?'

'Always.'

You say the word saudades, which has extra layers to the simple English of I miss you. Saudades, she says, muitas. You wonder if she is saying it about you or him. Just hearing the lovely swollen sounds of Portuguese come from your wife's mouth and throat and nose makes you miss Brazil. A decade you spent there and you remember arriving without a word of the language. To know nothing, nothing at all. Not even able to decipher the space between spoken words; they were all just a gooey flux of sound. And you were so timid in how you reached out your hand to introduce yourself. So embarrassed when they laughed and put their arm around you, or if it were a woman, hugged you and kissed your cheek. The smell of tangy summer in their touch;

in the very air around you. The cold, sugary sorbet of açaí, how good it tasted with strawberries and granola as the sun stretched prickly hot against the distant midday sky.

Mangoes. You used to wake up early while your wife slept. Before Ailish. Very early on, when waking up next to her naked meant you had to leave the bed. If not, you'd wrap yourself around her and wake her into sex. Mangoes always remind you of sex. Maybe that is why, instead of fucking you'd be skinning a mango and slicing it from its skin, sliding it from itself onto the plate. You remember how slippery a mango can be, how sweet. You think of who you were there, who you were before you went, and who you are now, and there is nothing you can see that links them. There is a part of you that wants to go back and a slice of resent for your mother slips from you before you can hold it back.

You drive back to the rented house. Each facade the same as you navigate through the estate. You've a sudden need to make something your own, to feel like it belongs to you and you belong to it. Katie is sitting on the couch in the sitting room.

'You're back early,' she says.

'Yeah, the teacher wasn't feeling well. We had to finish early.'

'Well, Ailish's fast asleep.'

'That's great, thanks a mil, Katie.'

'Not a bother, did you say you needed me tomorrow?'

'I did, yeah. Do you mind if I give you a buzz in the morning to make sure? Carolina might be coming back early.'

'Of course, I'll just get my jacket.'

She leaves and you realise you lied twice in thirty seconds. You go upstairs to Ailish's room and she looks toasty in the single bed with her blue bunny wrapped in one arm. You think you'll take her tomorrow, to see your mother. You have been visiting twice, even three times a week since she moved into the nursing home. It is easier to see her there, somewhere unfamiliar. The person she is now fits there. Not in the house you grew up in, with all those memories clashing against what she has become. You kiss Ailish on the head and close the door. Back in the kitchen you pour yourself a glass of wine from the unfinished bottle.

On the sofa you fiddle with the remote in your hand but do not turn on the TV. You remember the day Nina called you. The missed calls, then the voicemail. Her voice pounding down the phone. Telling you that something wasn't right. That she was going to the hospital, that she was so afraid. You listened to the voicemail in the toilet, on a break from a meeting. You ran from the office and pressed the button on the lift. You were on the fourteenth floor and by the time it arrived someone was asking you where you were going, that the negotiations were only beginning.

In the car, you tried to put the hospital address into Google Maps while swerving between cars. You thought you knew the way anyway and kept driving. Nina was just nervous. There had been a scan only a few weeks before and everything had been fine. The traffic was bad. The longer it took the worse you got. You searched the car for cigarettes, thinking you had some hidden somewhere. At traffic lights you screamed. You called Nina but no answer. Fuck, fuck, come the fuck on. You punched the wheel.

When you arrived, you parked on the street and abandoned the car. You entered through a car park, then a kind of workstation where every door required a card to scan. You saw someone leave one door and you ran through. It was a long corridor and the smell of disinfectant was overpowering. And there, just at eye-level, on one of the shelves, was a jar. And on it was your name. Bebê Maloney. The name struck you. You thought of your father.

Remembered seeing the post in the door when he was alive: Mr Maloney, and when he was dead: Mr Maloney, and your mother tearing at the envelopes.

It took you too long to realise that bebê was baby, and that the surname was not your father's but your own. Inside the jar floated something that reminded you of something you must have seen in a film about space or alien invasion. And still, you could not make the connection. Somebody opened a door and shouted at you in Portuguese and you left, asking for your wife, Carolina, you kept saying, Carolina Maloney, Carolina Moraes. Using all the names she had, until finally you were brought to her.

She was propped up against too many pillows and her belly was deflated and her face was strained pink and pale. A nurse tried to talk to you but you were falling to Nina, crying, saying, you're alive, oh, God, you're alive.

'It's ok,' she said, 'it's ok. Don't worry. It was twins, I just know it. I'm still pregnant Oisín, he's still here, he's ok.' She was holding her stomach smiling. And for a second you believed her and looked to the nurse who shook her head, slowly, so gently, but just enough. Just enough to know.

Then

Brigid was sitting at her desk and had been doodling in the margins of her History copybook for twenty minutes. Downstairs, her parents were listening to the news of the jubilee and she could hear her mother scoffing, or laughing a shrill fake whoop from time to time. One hand held a biro, the other made circular movements on her belly. A few months had passed since the wedding and, day by day, life had become more still. The first days after it she found it hard to be back at school, like she had transcended it. In class her mind would remember something new about the day, something that had eluded her before. James' hand squeezing her knee under the table as she tried to cut her steak. Her mother in the corner, as the dancing started, holding a glass of champagne in one hand, twirling a piece of loose hair around her finger and thumb with the other, smiling at the world.

And she'd replay the whole day in her head. From getting ready at home, to arriving at the church, seeing James all suited up with his hair slick back with gel, the wide smile on him, his hands fidgeting, going from his pockets to his waist to arms folded back to the pockets. Her father's arm in hers, his steady pace, his whisper in her ear, mo chailín álainn, mo stór. When she reached James, he took his hand in hers and it was wet with sweat. She blocked out everyone else, wanting to pretend it was just the two of them, just them and their baby. How quickly the ceremony went. Then the walk down to The Oyster Bay bar, which overlooked the harbour, with all the white tables and shiny cutlery, and the wedding cake, which Brigid's aunt had made herself. The size of it.

As those days passed by though, something else started filling inside of her. Thoughts she couldn't put words to. She had almost told James of them so many times, but always something stopped her. Christmas passed and the new year rolled in with all the thoughts opening up inside her in an almost tongue, and she thought if she could just sound them into the world they would connect and click together and the image of what she was feeling would become clear. She decided now, turning over a page in her copybook to write him a letter. She rolled up her sleeves and tied her hair loosely in a bun.

My wonderful James,

I am writing you a letter. It's silly, I know. Maybe I will not post it, and if I do, I will probably see you before you receive it. And I'll feel foolish. And I'll regret it, and yet I really want to try to make sense of everything going on inside my head. To put the words on paper and for you to read them alone and maybe in years to come you'll find this and read it again, and we will be in another time, maybe another place, and looking back we will say, it wasn't that bad. It wasn't bad at all. For look what we have now. The truth is, there are moments that I cannot wait to have what we will have.

I'm sorry for not asking you more about how you're feeling. About how these weeks have been, it's just what is happening to me is so momentous – it feels like with every day that I change, the world does, too. Subtle changes. The leaves fall as if being cradled. The sun, in the moments it breaks behind clouds has a voice, it is like the air around me hums. Even the water from the tap tastes crisper. Since the wedding it's like there is nothing more to think about apart from our baby. Also, and I don't want this to sound mean, or to belittle anything you might be going through, but everyone and all their issues are so distant now, so remote that I find it hard to remember how I ever cared. Because inside of me is our child. Our child. It is the most beautiful thing to think, that I have a child inside of me, and that we made it, and that one day we will hold him and he will be moulded by our love. It feels so unique, this feeling, yet I know it is probably the most universal of all feelings.

Of course, there are other times, normally in bed, that the darkness of the night outside is inside the room with me. And there is always that other life. I think it will walk side by side with us, that 'what could have been.' I know the training will be starting soon over in England, that you wish you were there. I know that, yet I'm glad you are here, with me. I think too of the person I thought I would become and if she will fade into something like a dream. If I will recognise her in myself at all in the future.

And the world, James, the world seems so small now. And my life so simple. And the news, everything that's happening up north, that poor baby blown to pieces in the car bomb, and I watched it with mammy and daddy and I thought of how we can protect our baby boy. Then all the other news that came after, no matter how important just seemed so silly. Isn't that terrible? And the two lads found shot dead in the car, I wanted to feel something so desperately but I didn't really even feel pity at the time, I just thought, how silly, how useless. It doesn't make sense to me, but on a different level now. It is as if it cannot penetrate me in any real way because there is this love, now; I see it almost as an armour. Of course, afterwards I thought a hundred other things and questioned what will come of the world. I spent the night wondering about the love I feel and the strength of it. And then I thought that if all mammies feel this, and all daddies, because I know you will feel this, too, then, if there's all that love, just so much of it, James, then how can a man shoot another man dead. Writing it now I get the urge to laugh at the senselessness of it.

I then thought of how I bullied poor Mary back when we were kids. In private, too, so no one ever saw. Not badly, now, but nasty in ways. And I thought then there must be a badness in me, a hate, I suppose, or not hate, but hate's friend, who walks hand in hand. I suppose some people are born with more of it. I don't think you were born with much at all, James, but you are an exception. I used think there was nothing of it in you, but the day you walked away from me, when I told you, I saw then that you weren't free of it either. I think everyone has it in them. And some of them never meet someone like you, or get the chance to have a baby, or some have no roof above their head, or have parents who beat them, or grandparents who abuse them, and then I thought that maybe the love isn't enough for all that. That it'd be too late by the time a boy is a man for love to have any real effect at all.

Do you ever feel these things? I was thinking here how I'd never be able to say all this to you, if you were sitting across from me. Firstly, I wouldn't have the courage, I suppose. Then you might interrupt. Or I might say it the wrong way and could offend you. It's just, I feel these things so intensely now. My thoughts are swirling all the time but they feel solely mine, for once. I feel like they really belong to me. I know I am thinking them. I know they are mine. Before I used to feel like I was just repeating something I'd heard, or maybe I was saying something for the sake of it, or if I thought something it wouldn't sound like my own thought, does that make sense? Like my thoughts were being thought inside my head without me. Now, though, I feel like I can think clearly. Even though my thoughts go so quickly now, and sometimes veer without warning, I know I am conducting their path. I am in the driving seat. It's because of our baby – the way I think now has purpose. Each thought is important because it is helping me to become a mother. That's what I think, like I'm on this intense and weighty lesson.

You must be reading this thinking I've gone half mad, and maybe I have. And besides, I've gone off point. The main reason I wanted to write to you is to tell you that I truly believe we will be fine. To be honest, I think we will be so happy, not that I am not now, I am, it's just I think our baby will just speed up all that love and happiness that was coming our way anyway. I thought I'd look down at this little pouch of a belly I have and want to hide it, but the truth is I do not. When I put my hands to it, I feel a calming pride. Your parents would be happy to know that it almost feels holy.

I have been thinking a lot about God, too. Not the God we read about in the bible, but a higher presence, because sometimes what I feel is so strong I think there must be something higher than us all. I am going off point again, I'm sorry. I was saying I do not care about what people think, I really don't. I know you do, and I know I did. We spoke so much about it. At the start I thought I'd die of shame – the looks and the whispers. It must be harder for you, I know. My parents being how they are and yours being how they are. You know what I think, it is only you that really matters.

How you see me. And even that, right now, with this mounting, cascading feeling of love I have for our child, even that does not seem important. Again, not in a bad way, I'm sorry if it sounds rude, or that you are unimportant. That is the furthest from the truth. It's just, I cannot give it much time because my thoughts move back to our baby.

James, we will have a baby and he will be brilliant and he will be loved so boldly and so wildly that I think the world will be better. That we will balance something out in the universe. That our love will tip the scales in a way. Our love for him – I know it might be a girl – but also our love for each other. I feel that changing, too. I love you wholly differently now to how I loved you a few months ago. So, I suppose that's the main point of the letter. To tell you that.

I love you, James.

Your mad Bridge.

She read it back over, stopping at certain parts, wanting to scribble through words or phrases. It wasn't what she had wanted to write and when she reread the part about love and hate and evil, she thought it sounded too easy, because her thoughts were so much more complex than that. She had tried to use words beyond her, had a list of words in a copybook she had taken from novels and poetry books, their meaning written next to them. How can we, she thought, again fiddling with the pen, sound what is in our minds, show ourselves, our real selves to someone else? How can I ever know someone else when I am only starting to know myself?

She put the pen down, leant back and lifted her t-shirt. Just below her belly button was where she could see the difference most. Protruding. Making himself known. She feathered her hand against the skin and hummed. She wanted to talk to him but was embarrassed to be heard. She had so many things to say, though. It is like a new language, she thought, that I can speak in a new tongue. She wondered what he'd look like, if he'd be as handsome as James, have his misty blue eyes, those dimples high up in his cheeks. He does not have to have anything of me, she thought, for he is connected to me and I to him, in a way that I will never feel again. She thought of how much she loved him already, although he was not yet the size of a pear. A sadness came over her then. He will never love me as much as I love him, she realised. Then she thought of how much she loved her parents and it was not the same as the love she had for the baby inside of her, and she imagined him being born, then five, then twenty and he would love her, but not like this. She imagined herself telling him, when he is about to be a father, now you will know, she'd say, now you will know how much I love you.

She put the pen down, pulled her t-shirt back down over her stomach and stood up. She folded the letter in two and hid it inside her notebook. She would get an envelope from town and post it later. Kathleen would drive Brigid and James into Cork in the afternoon for the scan. She thought of seeing the little foetus, the sound of the heartbeat echoing inside her.

She ate breakfast quickly. The conversation was normal. Tommy spoke about the land up by the Barrett's that had been sold to a construction company. Just imagine the number of houses going in there. And there's not road enough as it is! Brigid nodded and agreed. Kathleen said something from the sink about things evolving, the way of life. Then Brigid got ready upstairs and was already opening the front door when James reached out to knock. They kissed each other and went into the sitting room and waited for Kathleen. James' hand resting on her belly. The talk of boy or girl, names being thrown around. He liked Ailish for a girl and Oisín for a boy.

'Don't you think they both sound like the sea?' He asked. 'It's like a wave breaking or something.'

'That's nice,' she said, 'I mean about what you think of the names, not the names themselves.'

'Then what do you like?'

'Cian.'

'And for a girl?'

'Well, it's not a girl.'

'Ah come off it now, you can't be sure. We'll have to have a name ready.'

'Oisín,' she said, 'I don't hate it.'

Kathleen opened the door and told them hurry on up. Brigid knew she was agitated. She didn't like driving, especially in the city but Tommy was busy in the morning and had said, sure that's not something I could be doing anyway.

Any time they laughed or spoke too loudly in the car, Kathleen shushed them or said, for heaven's sake, I'm trying to concentrate. And she spoke badly of any car that overtook her, or that braked suddenly, and she outright cursed at young eejits who drove with the music blaring. She almost cursed at some posters up of the queen, with jubilee written in silver. She turned off the radio which was broadcasting it as they drove past city hall. Then as soon as she parked by Merchant's Quay her usual tone returned and she hurried them out of the car and said, we don't have all day you know.

Since the wedding Brigid was allowed to be more loving around James. They could kiss whenever they wanted and her parents would not complain. The rings on their fingers had aged them somehow and Brigid enjoyed it. They walked hand in hand, a step behind Kathleen all the way to the hospital, where they sat on plastic chairs until Brigid's name was called.

The doctor left Brigid and James in the small room, telling them he'd be back in a few minutes and for Brigid to take off her pants and lift her top and get under the blue sheet in the bed. James helped her and by the time the doctor came back she was in the bed, shivering a little.

'Now,' the doctor said, 'this is going to be a bit cold and I'll use this,' holding up something that looked like a torch, 'to find the baby.'

He wasn't old but his hair was greying. He had a large smile. Brigid looked at his hands and saw he was married. James' hand was in hers and when she looked at him his eyes were staring at the screen ahead. She breathed in nice and deep as the doctor squirted the cold gel on top of her belly and mushed it around, pushing the torch device in a little too hard by her hip.

'Now,' he said, 'see there? There we have two perfect feet.'

Brigid could see them, so tiny. And then they were gone, washed away in black and white until a hand appeared.

'One hand.' The doctor said. 'And the other, there!'

Brigid could hardly believe it. Her baby, with hands and feet.

'Now, we'll just listen to the heartbeat there now.'

He turned some things on the machine he was using, and the room swelled with sound. It sounded like a hundred heartbeats all at once, racing, racing to life. Brigid felt worried.

'Is it too fast? It sounds too fast!'

'It's perfectly normal,' the doctor said, 'a very strong heartbeat. Exactly what we want to hear.'

Brigid turned to James and he had tears in his eyes and more going down his cheeks. He looked at her and wiped his face with his other hand. He didn't say anything but exhaled loudly, making a whooshing sound.

'And here we have the little face.'

Brigid couldn't make out the features too well, and it kept moving, a flurry of blurs. She could just make out the mouth and it looked like James', wide and full. What a thing, she thought, to be alive. James squeezed her hand and the doctor pulled the device away and gave her paper sheets to wipe the gel away.

'A perfectly healthy baby,' he said and smiled at both of them. 'If you just get ready now Brigid, and you can go back to the waiting room then.'

'Ok, thank you,' she said, feeling the words silly and insufficient. There should be specific words for this moment, for the moment somebody shows another person their baby, making it real. When he left the room James stood up and started pacing.

'Jesus Christ, did you see? The little face!' He paced back and forth.

'I know,' she said, sliding off the bed and wiping the gel away and putting the paper in the bin. She put on her pants and jumper.

'He has your mouth,' she said.

'Do you think?'

'Sure of it.'

'Jesus like, it's mad isn't it.'

'It is.'

She put on her shoes and walked to him, holding him still. She kissed him and he kissed her back. He hugged her tight and she could feel his heartbeat, thick inside his chest, beating wildly against hers.

Now

Ailish has been sick on and off for two weeks, so you are both cranky from lack of sleep. Nina has been speaking about colleagues more and getting home later and going out for work drinks more often. Now you know what you're doing in the job, you have grown to hate it. There is the director, Philip, who is an academic and speaks down to you because you are not. Even though he is fucking useless. Then there is Caitlynn, who is also above you and is good at her job but cold and zero craic. She is waiting for Philip to retire. Then there is Maeve who you have to talk to on a daily basis, who you know is on the same pay scale as you but acts like she is not. She questions everything you do and says things like, well when I do that now, what I tend to do is...and then tells a long, boring story that could be simplified to a sentence. She is as plain as fucking cardboard and has a shrill voice.

Driving back into the university you play out little scenarios in your head that all end in you telling them they are a shower of wankers who can all go and get fucked. Mortgage. Just think of the mortgage. At traffic lights you look at the forms you got from the bank and feel defeated. Daft.ie is now your starred website and you refresh it three or four times a day even though no new houses you can afford come up. You're in foul humour and hope you don't have to speak to anyone in the office for fear of telling them to get fucked.

Parking the car, you take your phone out and text Rebecca. *Any other jobs going? I might be up for murder before my probation is done* 😉

You haven't spoken to her since the hotel and as you press send you feel like someone else. Sometimes you think you might be a sociopath. You're not really sure what a sociopath is but think you could be one. How you can just switch off to a life you love, to people you love and do horrible things and just be able to label it to someone else, something else. Is that sociopathic?

At your desk your phone buzzes. *Wouldn't look good leaving so soon after starting. But then wouldn't look good being a convict either. Ha! X.* You put your phone away and answer emails. You practice little phrases in Irish in your head. The classes are over but you still have your journals and books and there is something in learning the words that creates colours to memories. The more you speak little phrases to your mother, the more you can picture your father. Each word is like a little piece of stone and the more you say, the more there are, cementing themselves against each other, leading somewhere.

You take out your phone and text Nina. *How about a takeaway tonight?* You then go into Rebecca's message and delete all chat history. Nina texts back quickly. *Yes! Chinese* 😉

The rest of the day passes you by without having to talk to anyone in person, just emails and one Teams call. You leave a little early and drive to see your mother.

She is in the residents' lounge, which is just a large room with mismatched furniture and a bulky television that plays soaps too loudly. She is sitting next to a man called Francis. You've spoken to him a fair bit. He has one daughter who lives in Australia and sometimes you feel bad when you visit, knowing he has nobody. Depending on the day, you envy his daughter in Australia. You watch them from the double doors. She is laughing and seems aware of herself. He pats her arm with his hand. There is something tender in the touch and although you expect to feel something childish, you instead feel a warmth, knowing that when you are not there, she is with others and maybe her days are not like you have imagined. You walk towards them and speak a little to Francis. He says his daughter is coming in a few weeks and you say how happy you are for him. You help your mother up and then she slaps you away a little and walks with you side-by-side to her room.

'I was thinking,' she says, not looking quite at you, 'that you could bring some things into me, from the house.'

'Sure, like what?'

'Oh, up in the attic you'll find an array of trinkets. Bring in anything.'

'Ok, I will.'

'Have you been going there, watering the plants?'

'The odd time, yeah. I've been a bit busy actually, we're looking at houses ourselves, trying to organize the mortgage.'

'What houses? Your home is there, waiting for you. You know that small garden, when we first bought it, well...'

She is sitting in the armchair now, telling a story that is not connected to anything you know. You listen as she speaks words that juxtapose, words that when put together are a little off kilter

– they cannot carry their own weight. She loses herself in it and the frustration makes marbles of her eyes and she is picking skin at her fingers. She is slipping into her father's tongue and although you can now understand a lot of the words, the whole meaning is a blur, just hues of what the colour could be. When she strains her face, pleading for an answer, you say tá brón orm because you are sorry, for not being able to learn, for not being able to speak to her and calm whatever it is that troubles the essence of her. Tá brón orm you say because this is the way she will go, your mother, the woman who saved you endlessly. I wish you could just understand me, you say, I wish you knew how much I loved you. There's this paradox that I cannot figure out, but I think you'd have the answer if I could only understand you. You'd use words in the right order, you'd give them new meaning. Tá brón orm, a mham, you say.

She does not answer but looks out the window and you follow her gaze and birds fly by. You think they are chaffinches and then try to remember the collective noun for them, a flight maybe, or a band? It will come back to you, you hope. She turns to you and smiles. You smile back and she reaches out, so you move your seat forward. Now she takes your hand in hers and lifts it, placing it between her shoulder and cheek. She rests her head on it, closes her eyes and you want to really be there. With her. In this moment. But you cannot remember the name for a group of chaffinches. You are afraid that this is what will happen to you, little by little, forgetting fragments of who you are, of what makes you, you.

Then she takes her hands away from her cheek and she is trembling as she opens them, and you take your hand back. You think she will talk but instead she puts her hands on her lap and you see them, unsettled, unable to stay still. Then you remember, it is a trembling of chaffinches, and the memory of sitting on the bench in the garden with your father comes fully formed, as if you had remembered it a hundred times, his hand in yours, both of you looking to the sky as birds fly by and he says, did you know that groups of birds all have different names, and then he starts to list them as your eyes flick like wings, trying to take in the soaring, the sweep, the scope of birds flying; the freedom of it.

You are winded. You can see him, pointing, your eyes following his finger. There was a joke, he made a joke. What was it? He was laughing. You remember him laughing, head slightly back, did he slap his knee? His arm, reaching out to pull you closer to him but stopping. Then one of his hands grabbed the other arm. He made low rumbling sounds. You thought it was part of the joke, maybe. Get your mum. Those were the words he used. You can hear them, low, phlegmy, as he slid from the bench to the grass. You knelt closer to him. You didn't know, you were too young. But there is something there. You didn't want him to be alone. You were afraid. Your hands shaking as you tried to grab his arm. The sounds out of him. Your legs numb, curled under you as you lay on top of him. But there is something there. Then the sounds out of him getting lower and lower until there was nothing. The sounds of chaffinches in the sky. And his eyes. Looking out, beyond you, further, to something. And you turned your head to look but it was a grey sky with flicks of black flying back and forth and you tried to see something in the sky, a shape, a word from the birds that kept on moving, like everything was just out of focus and if you could just squint enough to see it, to see the message, but there was nothing. But there is something there.

'Oisín, mo pheata.'

You look at her and her face is confused. You put your head in your hands and you cannot stop the crying. It escapes from you in bursts of coughing and retching.

'Oisín, Oisín, what's wrong. Stop that now, Oisín. Come here to me, my beautiful boy.'

You cannot stand up from the chair. His face, his jaw slacken, his eyes. What were they looking at? What did you say? There is something there.

The door opens and you turn further in your chair so you cannot be seen.

'Brigid, supper! Oh, Oisín, how are you, I didn't see you coming in.'

You don't turn and you are unable to speak.

'Something's happened!' Your mother says. She is getting up from her chair. 'It's my granddaughter, something's happened to her!'

You lift your hand and shake it to try to contradict her but already you hear the tray being placed on a table and the nurse's hands on your shoulder.

'Oh God, oh God, what happened? Sit down Brigid, sit down there now.'

You look up and your mother is shaking and her hands wring themselves in an almost prayer. You stand up and walk to your mother and put your arms around her. You feel her arms around your waist and she smells like somebody else. There is nothing of her smell.

'Should I call someone? I should call someone,' the nurse is saying and you do not have the energy to say no, no, don't worry. You hear the door opening and closing. You release your mother and she too is crying.

'I'm sorry,' you say. 'I'm sorry. I couldn't remember.'

'Stop now,' she says. 'It's not your fault, whatever it is.'

You remember her coming out into the garden. You were cold

by then and shivering. You had not lifted yourself from him. You remember your right ear on his chest and the coldness of silence. You remember saying something. Or maybe he said more. Was that it, was that all he said, get your mum, or was there more? There is something there. What are ye at, is what she said, her voice behind you. And you jolted, guilty. You felt guilty. So, there is something there. Like when you stole a Mint Aero from Doreen's shop or pushed Jack down the steps. That was the first thing you felt. Guilt. And her voice, what are ye at, Oisín, Oisín, what's going on? Get up, Oisín. James! James, answer me, James. Go Oisín, she was saying, screaming, go Oisín, call an ambulance Oisín, and then pushing past you. And you lay back onto him. There is something there.

'I'm so sorry,' you say again.

'Stop now,' she says, 'stop now, sit down.'

You look at her again and kiss her forehead and hug her, then you turn away and walk out the door, down the corridor, out the front door and into your car. You sit there for a long time before there is a knock at the window and the nurse is asking you to open the door.

'I'm sorry,' you say, apologizing again, and again for the wrong thing, 'my daughter is fine, it's just, it's nothing. Sorry to have worried you.'

'It's your mum,' she says, 'she wouldn't stop talking about her granddaughter and then…you better come quickly.'

Then

The days were laden with worry, and those days stacked up into weeks, and the weeks into months of cement and brick around Brigid that at times felt like a home-to-be and other times felt like the unbreakable walls of a prison. She never sent the letter in the end but instead read it back to herself on the days when she'd come back from one of James' soccer matches feeling like she herself had been the ball being kicked around. Any matches now were teamed with scores of young girls from the other team, and all the girls who weren't in Brigid's class showed up, too. They weren't even the slightest bit subtle. If Brigid forgot herself and screamed when James scored, the girls would cover their mouths, some of them pointing, the others nudging, because now the bump underneath her clothes was protruding out into the world, making itself known. Lots of her own friends had distanced themselves from her. Talking to her in the corridor of school, or in the toilets, when other people were nowhere to be seen. Only Gwen had really been there for her since she started showing. On good days, she was happy about that – better to have one real relationship than ten superfluous ones. And it was real, the friendship between her and Gwen. It was becoming something sacred to Brigid.

On those bad days, when she'd cry and scream into the sheets, or the pillow, or a cardigan she had been wearing, her mother would say, oh, darling, it's all hormones. Brigid would spend afternoons lying in the bed with her mother. Both of them with books in their hands. Sometimes Brigid would doze off and often she'd wake with her mother's hands softly stroking her belly. Humming. On the days that her mother had chores to do or when she spent the late afternoons cooking, Brigid would feel a longing for her. Over the months she had told James she was too tired to do something or other, or she'd make up an excuse to him if her mother was at home with nothing to do, or if Gwen wanted to call round. There was something about talking to them that soothed her, their answers coming from a place of understanding, of mutuality. With James, she felt she needed to explain everything and it sapped something from her.

She lay in her mother's bed reading *Are You There God? It's Me, Margaret*. She had read it once already and this was the second time. It felt like a totally different book to the first time she read it and she couldn't understand why. Her mother had got it for her. Now, her mother had said, don't be telling anyone about it for heaven's sake, and just don't show your father, just to be safe. Brigid read about Margaret and Nancy, saw herself and Gwen. She even managed to contort certain scenery of the New Jersey suburbs into the pastoral paths to the village. Brigid was lying in her mother's bed wondering if she'd ever start talking to God when there was James' three-quick knock on the door. She clambered out of the bed arduously and walked to her room and

The Language of Remembering

put the book under her pillow before walking downstairs.

'They're starting to put the roof up, Bridge,' he spurted, then leaning round Brigid, shouted, 'Hi, Kathleen. They're starting on the roof today.'

The gravel, the stone, the concrete, the measuring and manoeuvring, was a great fascination to James, a fascination Brigid tried to get behind but failed. It was like the month before when Ireland beat France 1-0, and James was electric and buzzing around and spinning her, and she could feel the excitement, the pride of the moment, but it was felt only on the surface, like the heat of the sun through thick cloud.

Whenever she visited the site, it looked so dead, so cold. It's not a person like, James would say, it's not alive. Maybe that was it, the fact that it wasn't alive, that there was nothing of her in it. She'd been warned early on by her father not to interfere. Just let them go ahead with it now and be grateful, he'd said, and when she went to respond, he didn't let her. I'm serious now, Brigid, don't be interfering. So, she hadn't. And brick by brick, any fragment of a dream she might have had, became cold and grey inside her head. She'd look to her mother, who normally would have a bit of fight in her, or a wise word, but she'd just slowly shake her head. The one time Brigid had brought it up to her, when they were both lying in bed, she'd said, some fights aren't meant to be fought.

'Oh, marvellous,' Kathleen said, coming in from the kitchen. 'You'll really see a difference now.' She nudged Brigid a little as she moved behind her and walked up the stairs.

'That's great,' Brigid said and walked her way into the sitting room with James following.

'Don't you want to go over and see? I came over to get you.'
'I will, later.'

James sat down next to her with a face trying its best not to look upset or angry, or whatever he was feeling.

'It could be ready before the birth, I thought you'd be excited.'

'I am. It's great. Especially if we're in before he arrives. It's just like, let's call the house your baby.'

'What, and call our child yours?'

'No, I didn't mean it like that. It's just you can be excited for the both of us.' It was all she could give him.

'Grand.'

'Don't be odd, I'm just tired.'

'What's new?' he muttered.

She heard her mother's words about some fights aren't meant to be fought but be fucked with that, she thought, be fucked with the whole lot of them. She could feel the mood change so suddenly, like the misstep on a long, high tightrope and the moment of falling.

'Oh, I'm so sorry, James, I'm so sorry that I'm tired. It's just, you see, you might not have noticed but I'm the size of a fucking car and the child you put in me is draining all the energy I have. So I am ever so sorry that I can't do cartwheels around the fucking room because a roof is going up on a house I've had no say in from the start!'

God it felt good and horrible in equal measure. She was on her feet, pushing his arm away and at the bottom of the stairs, pushing the hair from her face with one hand holding on to the banister.

'Go off now to your roof!' she said climbing the stairs and before he could answer she shouted back, 'and the child you spoke of is grand by the way, in case you wanted to know.'

With that she closed the door to her own bedroom and leant against it to hear the closing of the front door below. She had hardly sat down on the bed before the door opened and her mother was looking at her in disbelief.

'Disbelief is it Mammy, or maybe there's a better word for it, incredulity, maybe?'

And with that Brigid started to cry, trying to hold it in, pushing her fist against her closed lips, but when she finally had to breathe in it was loud and telling, and only brought more crying. Kathleen sat next to her and draped an arm round her, pulling her in closer. Brigid thought her mother might say something, again some words, some knowledge that a mother passes down to a daughter, but instead she stayed quiet until Brigid was exhausted and had nothing left inside her.

'Now,' she said, standing up and pulling Brigid by both arms so she was upright too, 'go in and wash your face, put on some nicer clothes and I can drop you down to the house so you can see what all the fuss is about.'

'Mammy, I can't. I'm just so...'

'I know. I know you are. And wouldn't it be easier to lie in bed now until the baby comes, but that's fanciful and foolish and is not the way life is meant to be lived. Now, don't interrupt me, it's relentless and you're fatigued, but you'll just have to grin and bear it. It's your new home, it's where your child will grow up and where all their memories will be contained, so try to feign a smile at least.'

Kathleen steered Brigid into the bathroom with her hand on Brigid's lower back and closed the door on her. Brigid saw a chubby, cherried, ugly face looking back at her from the mirror. Her neck was thicker, so now when she looked down at herself a little roll had come between her chin and her chest. No wonder, she thought, he's looking at other girls on the sidelines. And only last week she saw him in the corridor talking to Emma and laughing his stupid head off. I wouldn't be a bit surprised, she thought, if he didn't end up in the house with her instead of me. Again, she felt like crying. She felt completely sure that this would happen and yet completely sure it wouldn't, and it was so exhausting, these conflicting certainties about everything. Gwen had told her how silly she was being, how at the match Gwen only saw James look for Brigid, sure hadn't he come right up as soon as the whistle blew to hug and kiss her instead of jumping up and down with his teammates. Gwen hadn't used the word paranoid but had circled around it in flowery paths.

She washed her face and brushed her teeth. Felt the baby move inside her, either telling her to sit back down or to get the hell on with it. She changed into a long green, flowery t-shirt and put on her dark green denim skirt. It was a nice, bright day and too warm for tights, but she put on a dark beige pair anyway, she didn't want James' mammy looking at her legs and then looking away, or turning away as she sometimes did. When she went downstairs her mother met her in the hall and said, my God, you'll be sweltering, Brigid. She didn't tell her to get changed but instead opened the door and waited for her to follow.

Kathleen drove up the driveway cautiously, and as they approached the house, which seemed a different house to the last time Brigid had visited, there was a small huddle of people, some looking up, and others pointing. Brigid could see James, and her parents-in-law, and another tall man who she'd met a few times now, who was running the show, Dan, or maybe Don, she couldn't remember.

'Tell them I'm off into town or something, I couldn't bare having to talk to them now.'

'Oh, and it's fine for me.'

'You've made your bed.'

Then as Brigid was getting out of the car, James' mammy was making her way towards them and Kathleen shouted from the car, sorry Aileen, rushing off into town, and then at just above a whisper, will you ever close the door, Brigid. The car drove off back down the driveway as Brigid walked towards Aileen. They never hugged, so Aileen's hand kind of hovered on Brigid's shoulder – the closest thing to affection she'd ever show.

'You must be so excited! We'll be relieved to hear the end of all the noise anyway, I can tell you that. Not that we mind, but it hasn't been easy. Poor David is slowly losing his mind, God help us, and James, too. He has a right knack for it, does my James.'

Brigid left her talking. Telling her how it wasn't any hassle for them at all, while all the while telling her how much hassle it was. And her golden boy was great at this, and he was even better at that, and on and on she went, so by the time Brigid had reached James she was angry with him all over again. When she slipped in next to him, he took her hand in his and leant in and whispered, I'm sorry, I'm an eejit I know. I'm sorry.

She squeezed him closer to her and looked up at the dormer bungalow that was a skeleton of a life that would be, and she felt a pang of happiness, for even happiness was conflicted now. She felt horrible for how she spoke to him earlier and worried the more she did it the less he'd love her. That maybe already she wasn't who she had been, and he was trying to figure out who she was all over again to see if he could love her. Jesus Christ, it was exhausting, the whole fucking trudge of it.

'Follow me,' he said, taking her hand and telling her to be careful, mind that now, just don't stand over there, and so on.

'This is the baby's room.'

She stood in the middle of it. The three walls stood incredibly close to each other, and the fourth wall was yet to be finished, and the door that would one day open the room lay against one of the walls. She tried to picture a little crib in the corner of the room. Imagined the walls plastered and painted and some pictures hanging on the wall. She tried to see herself leaning down with her son in her arms, placing him into the crib, singing, or humming, but the image was unclear, an out of focus haze of almost shapes.

'Well, isn't it great?'

'It is,' she said, 'it really is.'

'We'll be happy here Bridge, I swear we will. I can feel it. And one day we can sell it and move closer to the sea, and then maybe we'll have more kids, and then we can travel, and then I suppose we'll be old one day, but we'll be old together. What, what is it? Ah, Bridge, stop that now.'

'I'm sorry, don't mind me, I'm just a mess of emotions.'

His hands were wiping at the tears on her face, and she used the sleeve of her t-shirt for her nose.

'It's lovely. And far enough away from your parents, too.'

And she tried to laugh a little and James laughed a little back and said, come on, upstairs we go, just be careful now Bridge, hold on to me like.

Now

It has been almost seven weeks since your mother's stroke. November has brought darkness with it and Nina comments each day on how early the sun is setting. She starts work earlier than you to avoid traffic, and you have the daily arguments with Ailish about what gloves she will wear, trying to explain to her why she can't wear the pink sandals, showing her Mickey Mouse boots instead. All of a sudden, she has a personality, and it is fiery. You try not to laugh at her crossed arms and pout. Not funny, she screams, and you say sorry, it's not, I know.

You have taken the day off to take your mother to the hospital. She needs another scan. Ailish is ready, holding the banister as you walk down the stairs, saying, look, I do it myself. You're getting so big, you say, my big girl. Yeah, I'm massive now. At the bottom of the stairs you lift her up, open and close the front door and bundle her into the cold car. In the rearview mirror, she is looking out the window and she is bigger, her face rounder and she has a look about her. You think that one day you might remember this image and think about time and probably be angry about a thousand things, but now, bringing her to crèche, you feel at ease about all the things that will go wrong. She exists. And it is more than you can take in.

You pick your mother up, or rather, she is brought out and helped into your car. You haven't put music on, but her fingers roll a rhythm on her thighs. She hums a little. The nurses have said since the stroke she is talking less and less. Her movement is hindered but she can still walk but chooses not to. The doctors have told you that it might not be the only stroke, that it is common for patients to have more. They have increased her medication, are trying to bring her blood pressure down, and tell you not to worry.

'Any idea what you'd like for Christmas?'

She looks at you, uncertain of something and turns to the window.

The humming changes to Oh Holy Night.

'I thought maybe we could go for lunch, maybe down to The Anchor if you're up for it, before Christmas? Me, you, Nina, Ailish and Granny?'

She continues humming and you sing the words in your head. *Fall on your knees, Oh hear the angel voices.*

As you are arriving at the hospital your grandmother calls you.

'You're delayed!'

'What?'

'I'm here waiting! Exasperated trying to find you.'

'We're arriving now. I didn't know you were coming.'

'Oh, of course you didn't. Convenient.'

'We'll be in the main entrance there in about three minutes.'

'Fine, fine,' and she doesn't hang up so you hear her conversation go on with God only knows who, 'he's always been tardy, distracted to high heavens is my grandson.' You hang up then and look at your mother and she wears a wry smile.

You and your grandmother wait while your mother is wheelchaired off for scans.

'Well, how is the job?'

'It's grand.'

'Grand, that's a euphemism for what exactly?'

'It's not a euphemism for anything. It's grand, like. I don't love it, but it will get us a mortgage and that's what matters.'

'And what about your mother's house? What about my house?'

'What about them?'

'Well, we're not going to live forever. They'll only be yours.'

'Stop with that talk will you.'

'With what talk? The truth. Sure, I don't have long left, I could go any day now, and your mother won't be going back home, would you not just move in there?'

'I couldn't. Look, will you stop. It'll be grand.'

'Grand. If there's a word ever to be overblown and over-stated in this country, it's grand. Fatigued to death is the word. And subjugated to all meaning except the very meaning it was given.'

You laugh a little and she nudges you.

'Tell me about the job for heaven's sake, before I lose my mind in this room.'

'It's...' you smile, 'it's just not what I wanted. The people I work with are almost toxic. I find it hard to be in their company.'

'So are you going to just acquiesce?'

'I don't speak French.'

'French?'

'I don't know what acqui whatever means.'

'Acquiesce, its etymology is Latin. It means to idly accept, to consent, to not bloody stand up for yourself is what it means.'

'Well, sorry.'

'Now don't get angry. What I mean is who even are these people and what will they ever mean to you? Don't let inconsequential people have such power on your wellbeing.'

'I know. It's just the stupid mortgage.'

'Just move into your old home, there's a solution waiting.'

'I told you, I can't. I couldn't.'

'Fine, fine. And how is Carolina? And my lovely Ailish?'

'They're great. Nina is working a lot. Ailish suddenly has a personality.'

'Oh lovely.'

'You know you can come visit whenever you like?'

'Thank you. A phone call to invite me on a specific day would be nicer. I don't want to trouble you. Better still, why don't you come for lunch or dinner to my house one day?'

'You don't have to be worrying about cooking for us.'

'I'd like nothing better.'

'Ok, great.'

'How about Sunday?'

'Yeah, that should work. I'll just have to check with Nina.'

'Perfect. I'll start thinking about the food. Let's say 3pm?'

'Great, great.'

The rest of the waiting is littered with spurts of chat and long silences. When your mother is finally rolled back out, your grandmother is asleep and you stand up silently. The nurse takes you aside and tells you that it took longer because your mother was very restless and wouldn't stay still.

'She started crying but we were able to calm her down. The results will take a few days but if you have any other questions before then, there is a number to call in here,' and she hands you over an envelope that you take with a smile. You walk back over to your mother and lean down to her.

'Are you ok mum? Was it ok?'

'Dreadful.' She says.

You smile because it is the first word she has said in so long. You wake your grandmother up and she shoots up off the chair and takes hold of the handles of the wheelchair and pushes your mother out in front of you, talking about how hospitals really need to do something about waiting rooms.

At home, that evening, you open wine and cook garlic chicken and pasta in pesto sauce. Ailish eats quickly and says she's tired and then fights when you bring her up to bed. She sleeps quickly and you leave the white noise playing as you close the door. When you get downstairs, Nina has lit candles and there is slow jazz playing.

'I like it,' you say.

'Siri's choice.'

'She's got good taste to be fair.'

Nina laughs a little and puts her arms around your waist and her head against your chest. You both sway a little without speaking. You imagine that you can see the scene from above. Wine on the table, candles lighting, sheets of a child's painted paper scattered, a couple swaying. Then Nina pulls away and sits down at the table and you do the same.

'You don't open up to me anymore,' she says.

'Of course I do,' you say, knowing you don't. 'It's just we've been busy, you've been working loads, and with mum and stuff, I don't know. Sometimes I don't want to talk.'

'I miss you.'

'I'm right here,' and you reach out your hand and she takes it.

'I know, that's what makes it worse.'

Nina is looking at you and she is not angry. She is not trying to annoy you or pick a fight. You can see it in her, she misses you. She looks a little lost.

'I'm sorry. I've been really shit. I'm sorry.'

'I just want you to talk to me. Tell me what the fuck is going on in there. Why are you shutting me out?'

'It's so stupid. I'm just a little insecure. And the house thing is just driving me crazy, like. It's nonstop in my head. You'd never cheat on me, would you?'

'Are you joking?'

'I really wish I were.'

'I would never do that. You know that. I think you're deflecting, you're like saying that because it's something you would do.'

'I wouldn't.'

She looks away.

'There's my parents' home, you know. I can't even visit the place. Gran was saying that like we should move in there.'

'It's not a bad idea.'

'I don't know, it would be so weird. I feel like there's too much there, too much happened. The place makes me feel guilty.'

'Guilty?'

'Yeah, and there was mum's stroke. I just keep thinking about it you know, like it's my fault.'

'How could it possibly be your fault? She's sick.'

'I think I stressed her out. Like, made her worry and then her blood pressure or something.'

'It wasn't you.'

'Nina?'

'Yes.'

'I think it was. We were having this lovely moment and then I remembered my dad, you know. Like, I remembered the day he died, so clearly. And I could never remember it. Every time I tried it was like a fucking blur, or like I couldn't push it further, I don't know how to explain it. And I was with her and I broke down. I just couldn't stop crying.'

'Why didn't you tell me? It's ok, it wasn't your fault.'

'She thought it was Ailish. She thought there was something wrong with Ailish. She was crying and completely frantic and I just left the room. I couldn't stay there.'

'I thought you were with her when it happened? You said you were with her.'

'I wasn't. I went to the car and then the nurse came and told me. I left her in a state thinking something had happened to Ailish. I think it was like the catalyst or something.'

'Hey, hey,' she is on her feet and leaning down with her arms around your shoulders and kissing your cheek and eyes and lips, 'it wasn't your fault.'

You want to tell her about the memory of your father. You want to voice it out. You want to admit it, that you are guilty. You want to tell her that if you lived in that house, it would be there, the memory, every day. You want to say the words out loud but she is kissing your lips and you are opening your mouth and standing up and nudging her towards the island. She is leaning back and sitting up and biting your bottom lip. Your hand is opening the button on her pants and pulling the zip down and pushing beneath.

'It's so cold,' she says, 'can we go upstairs?'

You both hurry, taking your wine glasses and closing the door gently and tiptoeing the carpet stair. She is first under the blankets and she wriggles herself free from clothing. You get naked and climb under and there is a heat off her. Everything is warm and soft. Slowly, contently, everything else leaves and the taste off her is all there is. Soon, you both forget that Ailish is asleep in the room opposite and you feel that you are young, and it feels like fucking when fucking was just that and there was no responsibility or afterthought. You sleep the whole night through for the first time in weeks and when you wake Nina is still in bed, looking at you.

'I took a sick day. Do the same.'

'Ok.'

'Good. Get Ailish ready and we can drop her to crèche and head off for the day.'

'Ok.'

'Good,' she says and is kissing you again. You feel the shift of something, like a large sea mammal has opened up its mouth and is spitting you back out.

You drop Ailish to crèche, she runs into the room without looking back and when you get home, Nina is dressed and ready to go.

'Where are we off to, then?' you ask.

'Your parents' place. Don't even, let's go. Didn't you say your mum wanted stuff? Come on, let's go.'

Inside, the place is musky. You pick up the letters that have gathered while Nina goes into the kitchen.

'Jesus Christ!'

You walk in and she is holding her nose with the fridge open.

'Seriously, you couldn't have emptied it all out.' She is taking a bag of black carrots out and throwing them in the bin. You open the kitchen window and the back door that goes out to the garden. Nina empties the fridge while you empty the cupboards. You work together without talking. Once she has cleaned the fridge and you have binned the cereal boxes, gone off spices, even tuna cans that are out of date, you boil the kettle and you both drink black coffee at the kitchen table.

'It's not a bad size, you know,' she says, standing up and walking out the back. You stand up and follow her.

'And if we wanted, there'd be room to extend out. There are houses further up that built a second story, too.'

You picture Ailish running in the garden. Is there a way for new memories to smother the older ones, giving them no space to aggravate?

'I don't know. I can't explain it, but I just can't see myself living here.'

'Here, in the now? Or in the house you grew up in? They're different, you know they are.'

And what, you think, is the past, and does it exist at all? Just memory, and even then, that is only a version, a long stretch of almost images with a faint sound that are more dreamlike than reality.

'I know. Would you actually like it here?'

'I would.'

'I just don't know if it would ever feel like home, again.'

'Oisín, it's just brick and carpet. It's the people, you know that – it's the people that make it a home. We would make it a home.'

You smile at her and walk back inside. It would need a new kitchen, and the floors would need ripping up. The downstairs toilet, too, everything dug up and thrown out. You walk into the sitting room and Nina follows.

'I'm going up into the attic,' you say.

'Ok, I'll organize down here.'

You find the ladder and climb up, using your phone as a torch until you find the light switch, but it doesn't turn anything on. Your eyes adjust to the darkness and the steady glow from the phone, and you open boxes, unrooting parts of who your parents were. There are letters, and photos, and poems, and clippings of The Irish Times and The Irish Independent. Pictures of a house under construction, not this one, but one surrounded by fields. There are books with writing on the inside, your mother's name, a date, her handwriting not too different to what it is now.

You read one of the letters. She is pregnant with you. When you finish it, you start from the top and read it again. There is a sense of tethering, of interweaving. The whole notion you had, of things you believed fundamentally missing, were there all along. Things are in context, in perspective, and you fold the letter up and put it into a box in which you have gathered anything that might bring a smile to your mother's face, anything that might bring something new to the surface and, by doing so, maybe coil the loose threads tighter together, making of them something new, something beautiful.

Then

Brigid started with the headaches not long after the roof was put up, when they were plastering walls and hinging doors, and asking Brigid about colours and then ignoring her, or saying, a little ambitious now for a small house like this. She didn't say anything about the pain at the start. Sometimes they'd be so bad her vision became a blur, like she was wearing prescription glasses. Kathleen knew something was up and more than once said she should call the doctor, but Brigid told her not to worry, that she was just tired. She'd run out of words for how she felt. Was sick of hearing her mother say fatigued, or bedraggled, or worn out, washed out.

She was walking with James up and down her road, trying to exercise. She was embarrassed by herself and when she said as much, James just laughed and said the fresh air was doing him good, too.

'You don't have to be worrying much now, sure, about Mr O' Callaghan and the fecking exam he has planned for us next month.'

'I suppose I don't.' She heard the sadness in her voice and wasn't expecting it.

'I didn't mean it like that, not like…'

'I know you didn't. I didn't think I'd miss his exams. I suppose it's just the end of school really for me now. Like, I won't go back or anything.'

'Why not, like you could still do the leaving?'

'Will you come off it. With a baby, no, it's ok. I'll just miss it is all. The chats like.'

James held her hand and she'd left him wordless again. A newfound talent. That and bringing the conversation in a surly, sour direction without exactly knowing how.

'Do you need help with English?' Brigid said, forcing her voice up, trying to make it sound blue and open.

'Wouldn't it be great if you could just do that exam for me? It's like I have the words in my head but getting them on paper is another thing.'

'You're great with words. Have you any new poems?'

Again he went silent. The times she'd bring up his poems he'd say, ah that was a silly phase, or, that was nothing, will you stop bringing it up.

'Wouldn't it be nice,' she tried again now, 'in years to come for Oisín to read them. To know something about it all. To know we loved him?'

'You should write some, you'd be brilliant.'

'I've written him letters, is that strange?'

'Have you?'

'Yeah, I just wanted him to know that we have always loved him, like, in case anyone tried to say different. Or if he thought anything, he'd know.'

'I understand that. I have written a few lately, it's just I don't know what they're really saying.'

'Show me. Will you, please?'

'Ah, they're not good now, Bridge. I don't understand them myself.'

'Please?'

'Grand, I'll show you. What, now?'

'I'm getting tired anyway, you can bring them back here, can't you?'

Brigid could feel the familiar throbbing behind her eyes.

'Grand so, let me walk you back.'

'No, don't be silly. Go on off there now.' And she waved him away and started walking back up her own driveway, the pain more acute now. She held against the wall of the house to get to the front door and opened it, going upstairs slowly, one hand on the banister, the other grazing against the wall. In her room, she got into bed and under the covers and put a pillow over her face to block any light.

Her mother came in and sat at the bottom of the bed.

'Oh, she's actually coming, can you believe it? The pure ludicrousness of it all. Can you imagine what it will do, the protests? I mean can you imagine her stupid little wave along the painted curbs? Jesus Christ, I'm telling you, it'll bring more ruin to the place.'

As Brigid moved to turn on her side, she felt a pang right under her ribs, it was sharp, hot, and she knew something was wrong. She was afraid to move. Her mother was putting things away in the wardrobe now, lost in her own monologue.

'Loyalty and friendship, I swear, she wouldn't know the meaning of either.'

Brigid was afraid of any movement, hurtfully aware of her own body and the ways it could betray her. Mammy, she tried again, Mammyyyy.

Kathleen turned round, still with a pile of clean clothes.

'Where will I leave these?'

'Mammy, something's not right.'

Kathleen put the washing down on the floor and Brigid saw the neatly folded pants and cardigans fall over in a small silent slump.

'What is it, what's wrong?'

'I felt something, really sharp. Something's not right.'

Kathleen lifted up the blanket from Brigid and looked down and in that movement Brigid saw her whole face change and Brigid's future with it.

'What is it mammy?'

'It's nothing love, just a tiny bit of blood. It's normal now, stay calm. I'll just go downstairs quickly, now just stay there and take deep breaths.'

Brigid did as she was told but as soon as Kathleen had said the word blood, she could feel something hot between her legs and wasn't sure if she was imagining it or not, but she felt like it was oozing, she could feel it all down her thighs. Then her whole arm started tingling and she thought she might be having a stroke, or a heart attack, which one did you feel the arm on? She knew she was going to get sick and couldn't move in time and she vomited all down the front of herself, just as Kathleen was coming back in the door. Brigid could feel sweat tickling the top of her ears.

'It's ok, it's ok.' Kathleen had a towel and was slowly wiping the sick from Brigid's chin and t-shirt. Then she had a cold cloth against her forehead and it felt brilliant and sent a chill down the back of her neck. My hands, Mammy, she thought she said, and could see her wrists swollen.

'Shhhh, you're going to be fine. Daddy is on the phone to the doctor now, he'll get the car ready and we'll drive you straight into the hospital, you can lay down in the back seats. Easy now, don't be crying, love, you're ok.'

'Am I losing him, mammy? Am I going to lose him, am I?'

'You are not, you're fine. Just might be coming a little sooner than thought, that's all.'

'I'm scared, mammy.'

'I know, love, I know. I'm here, don't worry now, I'm here.'

'I love you, mammy, so much.'

'I know that, love, I know all that. You're fine now. Look, Da is on his way up, we'll help you down.'

Tommy hadn't shaved that weekend and when he came into the room there was something about the grey hair building at his neck that made him look terribly old, and it was this, with no idea why, that made Brigid most upset. That even if everything was ok, even if her baby boy was fine and she was fine, that one day she'd lose her daddy, and her mammy, and she thought that life was just fierce cruel, even in the good moments, even when you were happier than you could ever be, life was cruel, because you knew it couldn't last, you knew, deep down, that you'd no control over any of it.

'Daddy,' she was saying and that was all she could say because she started crying and thought that maybe she could die, sure hadn't it happened before, hadn't her mammy's cousin died in childbirth.

'Hush now, my cailin ban. You're ok, my darling girl, you're ok. Link your arm in mine there now, there you go, sit up a little bit there, exactly like that, perfect.'

Then there was a knock on the door. Kathleen was up and out of the room and she could hear her talking and James' voice, then a pounding on the stairs and James was bursting through the room. He was holding a bulk of paper in one hand that scattered and swayed to the floor as he rushed to her side. He didn't say anything. Unlike her father, he looked much younger, just a boy. The big eyes already flitting about, to her waist, to her legs, to her face. He linked her other arm, and she could see his eyes mad inside his head and the sheer panic behind them betraying any sign that things could be ok.'

She lay in the back of the car, her head on James' lap, and he stroked the side of her head. She could feel something between her legs and thought it must be a towel.

'My hands, James, what's going on?'

'They're grand, you're grand, I promise. You'll be grand.'

'James, if something happens...'

'Stop, stop will ya. Nothing's going to happen, I swear it won't.'

'I know, but, you know I love you James, I really do. Sorry for the last few weeks, I am.'

'Stop, really now. Kathleen, tell her will ya, tell her to stop.'

Kathleen leaned around from the passenger seat and reached her arm to Brigid and took her hand, rubbing it with her thumb.

'James,' Brigid said again, low so he had to lean a little closer. 'If something happens to me, James, you'll take care of Oisín, you will now. And you won't let your parents force religion on him sure you won't? You'll bring him up reading what he wants, won't you James?'

'Will you stop, Bridge, really, stop, please.' James' words got stuck somewhere in his throat and he made a horrible groaning sound that he tried to pass off as a cough. Brigid was not aware of her body anymore and she felt herself at the edge of sleep. She thought of all the days that would hopefully follow this one. She was aware of wanting it to be over, whatever that meant. Wanted this passage of time to not exist at all, or for it to be so far in the past she could talk about it anecdotally, could imagine James butting in saying, ah I wasn't that bad now, or, it wasn't like that, sure you were out of it, so you were. That was the last thing she could remember and when she woke she was in a ward with eleven other patients and the sound of people speaking, and machines whirring and beeping, and doors opening and closing, was so intense that she could feel a pain coming out of her eyes.

The next time she woke it was dark and opening her eyes was easier. Her mouth was so dry and she tried licking her lips and bringing spit up to wet her tongue. When she looked to the side, her mother was sitting on a chair and her eyes were closed.

'Mammy.' Her voice sounded adrift in a wind.

Kathleen's eyes shot open and she stood up quickly, knocking the book from her lap.

'Oh, Brigid, are you ok? You look ok.'

'Water, mammy.'

Kathleen picked up a cup from out of Brigid's sight and held it to her mouth. The water was lukewarm and trickled down her chin and neck. She slushed it around her mouth and then swallowed more and more. When Kathleen took it away, Brigid said, more, mammy, please. She drank what was left in the cup and closed her eyes again, feeling her mammy's hand in hers.

'What happened, mammy, is Oisín ok?'

'He's fine, my love, he's fine. It's all ok now, just a bit of a scare.'

'I'm so tired, mammy.'

'Close your eyes, relax now. James only just left, he'll be back.'

Brigid closed her eyes but didn't sleep. She could hear her own breath coming as a slow scratchy wheeze. Kathleen pulled her chair closer and one hand held Brigid's and the other was pushing hair behind Brigid's ear, and rubbing her temple softly. She heard her mother talk, and later she wouldn't remember if it was a dream or not, but her mother's voice was soft at her ear, don't ever do something like that to me again Brigid, I couldn't handle it, my girl, my darling, darling girl.

Brigid slept until the early hours of the next morning and when she woke it was James who was sitting in the chair.

'Morning,' he said, dragging the chair closer to her. 'Don't worry about speaking now if you're not up to it.'

'I'm grand,' Brigid said, lifting herself up against the pillows. 'What happened?'

'The doctor said he'd be by soon, will I get a nurse?'

'Sure can't you tell me?'

'Lots of big words, Bridge, I can't remember them. But you're fine, the baby's fine. Just complications is all. High blood pressure. There's a name for it. It's why you're swollen and all that.'

'Is it something I did? Did I do something wrong?'

'Stop out of that will ya, course you didn't.'

'Can I go home?'

'I'm not sure, I don't think so, Bridge.'

Brigid shifted her head to take in the ward. Lots of single beds with sheets around them, like shower curtains. She could see a slit between the one around her bed and could make out another woman across from her sleeping. She could see the bump. She looked much older than Brigid.

'Is everyone pregnant in here?'

'I think so, yeah.'

'I must be the only child among them I suppose. They're probably all talking about me, are they?'

'Don't be silly, Bridge, sure how are they to know anything about you.'

'The nurses hate me I bet. I want to go home, James, can you see if I can go home?'

'Relax there now, I'll get a nurse. Just wait now, they'll be able to tell you.'

James disappeared behind the sheet and she saw the other woman fully for a second. She looked like she was meant to be pregnant, and everything around her seemed in place and ready. Brigid held her own belly and spoke softly to Oisín, saying, don't worry, my darling boy, don't worry about anything. I've got you, I love you.

Now

Christmas is cold and the house is full of music and Ailish asks each day, in the build up to the big day, if tomorrow is, in fact, the big day. You make a calendar with her, you try to teach her the days of the week and slowly realise she has no grasp on time and you speak to Nina about how beautiful that must be. Say, wouldn't it be great if we were all like that? To which she smiles a little. January brings a mortgage approval in principle, and the first two weeks of the month are the nicest you can remember since moving home. The money will be spent refurbishing your parents' house while your own rented house now is littered with kitchen magazines, and bathroom catalogues, and Nina has printed off photos of rooms she loves from Pinterest, and they too are scattered on the table, in the toilet, on the sofa. The awkwardness and looking away between you and Nina has bloomed back to late night touching and plans for the future.

You still have the two boxes you took from the attic in the car and every time you visit your mother, you want to bring them in, but first you see what kind of mood she'll be in, and she is never really in the mood – either complaining about pain, or not wanting to get out of bed, or repeating herself in rapid fashion, her short-term memory in chaos, or she hums and sings lullabies as Gaeilge, or she speaks as Gaeilge and you do your best to answer, only for her to think you are her father, and then she spends a long time apologizing.

Today, though, you will take them in and you will tell her the news. About the house. The plans to build a second floor, a room for all the books. You tried twice before to tell her, hoping she would say that it made sense, that it was judicious, or to say that she was fulfilled. Instead, when you tried, you heard her take a deep breath that almost made a humming sound, then that awful sound of tongue on teeth over and over.

In the car on the way up you call your grandmother.

'Darling,' she says, 'are we still on for Sunday?"'

'We are of course.' For weeks now Sunday lunch in her house has been a regular. Ailish loves it, the big garden, the treks around the countryside, the horses and cows. You walk with her in the cold, hats and scarves, imagining how your mum and dad had walked the same small roads.

'Marvelous. Have you told poor Brigid about the house?'

'On my way up there now.'

'That's good. That'll cheer her up, it really will. I do have something to say though.'

'Go on.'

'Well, it's not favourable, unfortunately. Do you know Angela Rice, do you know Rice's farm?' And before you can answer. 'No? Well, he died a few years back and she's the wife. A protestant of course, an abundance of land and property and money. Now, I've heard from your other grandmother, who still wants you to call, and from other people, that she now owns all the land up behind the garden and that she has plans for it and is bound to put an objection in about your planning permission.'

'Seriously? But like, there's no view to block, nothing to object to.'

'I know. I didn't want to tell you. I just didn't want you to be too buoyant.'

'Ok, thanks.'

'You should call your other grandmother, she wants to talk to you.'

'Yeah, I will.'

'Ha. You're no stranger to beguiling. See you Sunday.'

You hang up and think of your father's mother. She was not a presence in your life and when she was, she was strict and harsh. You remember the roughness when she cut your nails, sometimes drawing blood. You remember the short nasty words. To you. To your mother. Once, during that period when words were all a tangled web of misunderstanding, she took care of you in her house for a night. Your mother must have needed a night free. She sat you down on one of the kitchen stools and put a book in front of you. You cannot remember the exact words she spoke but they were sharp, cloaked by a soft tone and a hand rubbing your back. Soon the hand stopped rubbing and the cloak drooped to the floor like tar, and her voice took a shrill, screechy tone. Then her hand slapped you across the back of the head. Then she sat across from you and said you were breaking your mother's heart and your poor father in the grave, what would he think? Then she shouted READ! And when you tried and couldn't, she slapped you hard across the face and told you to go up to bed. It was early and you walked up the stairs and into the spare bedroom and watched the sun set and your stomach grumbled until you fell asleep. You woke in the morning and as you walked down the stairs you heard her talking to your mother, telling her ye had a lovely night, how you hounded down roast spuds and chicken, and how she tried to teach you solitaire.

Your phone rings and you answer.

'Hello?'

'Hi, it's me. Everything ok?' Nina asks. Ailish is singing in the background.

'Yeah, sorry, didn't see it was you, was lost in my own thoughts.'

'About the house?'

'About my grandmother, my dad's mum.'

'Really?'

'Yeah.'

'Are you going to call her?'

'She slapped me once, right across the face because I couldn't read.'

'Jesus. Was she always like that?'

You are pulling into the nursing home and park around the side.

'I don't really know. All my memories of her are kind of spun from that one. It's stupid like, but I feel like it's the last way I can stay loyal to mum or something. You know? Like, she was always so mean to my mum.'

'It must be hard. But it was a long time ago. She was grieving too.'

'Yeah, I know. Maybe I'll get gran to invite her on Sunday? I'm allergic to be honest, but sure...'

'I think it's a good idea.'

'Yeah.'

'Anyway, will you pick up a few things on the way back, I'll send a list by text now.'

'Of course.'

You hang up, get out of the car and take one of the boxes from the boot and head inside. Your mother is sitting on the armchair in her room and there is a newspaper open on her lap but she is looking out the window.

'Hi, mum. How you doing?'

The nurses have told you that she responds better now to shorter, simple sentences. One focus of a conversation. And it helps when you get her to look at you, instead of like this, out the window. You drag the chair and sit across from her.

'You doing ok?'

She turns her head to you and holds her shoulder and grimaces a little.

'Is it sore?'

She nods and you stand up and rest your hand on her shoulder, rubbing it, softly. She smiles and you pull the box over so it is in between both of you, so that you can reach down and pull things out while also being close enough to take her hand.

'I brought some things from home.'

She looks down at the box and you pick up a notebook. It is filled with lines written by your father, some scribbled out, others scribbled over, and among the pages are full stanzas.

'There are some of dad's poems here, will I read one?'

She doesn't say no so you start reading aloud.

There is a calmness to the day yet to start,
Birds quiver and shake themselves from branches,
The neighbour's dog lets out its first bark, scattering
More movement from above. You are still asleep,
And I wonder what you dream of, and if you'll be happy
To wake to this new house, not yet a home.

'That was when we moved,' she says. She's smiling.

'Moved to the bungalow?'

'Silly of him, he knew how happy I was.'

'Will I read another one?'

'What's that?' She's pointing to the folded paper, ripped from a copybook.

'Your letters.'

'Oh, I never sent them. Always too afraid.'

'They're beautiful mum, you write so well.'

'I was afraid, a long time ago, for a long time, I was so afraid.'

'I know.'

'And for what! Look at you now.'

'We're going to stay in the bungalow mum, in your house, if that's ok?'

She takes your hand and you stand up and sit on the arm of the chair, her head rests on your chest.

'Of course it is. I can't see why you wouldn't. A house by the sea, it's all I ever wanted.'

'We're trying to get it all sorted now, I'm talking to a lawyer and stuff. But maybe next week we can go there, take you out for the day, if you're up for it?'

'Oh, that would be nice, wouldn't that be nice? Your father will love it.'

You take a photo album from the box and open it up on your lap, turning the pages slowly. You move them without talking, giving her enough time to take in the faces frozen in time. When you close the album, she is sleeping. You put the box next to her armchair and as you are leaving, you tell the nurse that maybe it would be good for someone to read her something from the box each day.

'James?'

You turn and your mother is trying to stand up. You go over and help her up and she links your arm.

The Language of Remembering

'Can we please just get out, please, can we just please! Please!'

She is shouting and the nurse comes over and helps her on the other side.

'It's a little cold, Brigid,' she is saying, 'how about we go to the residents' lounge?'

She says it as if it is something grandiose, chandeliers and marble floors.

'I can take you out, mum, would you like that? Wrap you up warm?'

'Oh, yes, yes.'

You and the nurse help her into the wheelchair and wrap her in blankets, her arms stuck under the weight of them. You push her out into the garden, down the path, to a large silver birch. There is a bench and you sit down. Looking up, the branches are all bare, shooting up as if reaching for something. The clouds give nothing back.

'Sure you're not too cold, mum?'

'Oh no. It's fresh.'

She is facing you so your knees almost touch. Her body is friable. It makes you think of a Digestive crumbling into tea, not being able to hold the weight of itself. You reach out and rub her legs and she smiles.

'I miss so many things,' she says.

'I know.'

'Driving fast!'

'You? Driving fast? You were the slowest driver ever!'

'No, not me. James used to drive fast. Oh, the window was open and all that air.'

Her eyes are closed and she takes a deep breath. You stand up and walk behind her.

'Are you ready?' You ask.

'For what?'

'You'll see!'

And then you start pushing her, using the front of your feet to push forward, then your whole feet, and thighs and calves, so you are almost running, with your arms outstretched and your mother laughing against the wind, her thin hair falling behind her as you sway around the path, all around the nursing home, like a track, all the way back to the bench, and she laughs and whoops, once shouting, faster, another, oh, oh, careful, and you laugh too, and do one more lap until you are out of breath. It feels like you are playing a trick on time, or memory, and maybe that's the same thing – you are outrunning the past, rerouting it, a reversal of roles that remoulds something anew.

You push her slowly now back to the bench and sit down. Her face is smiling and there are windswept tears across her cheeks. She rolls her head backwards and looks up to the sky and lets out a low whistle that becomes part of the wind and whittles away.

On the way home you buy carrots and some other things, a small bouquet of flowers, some nice champagne and Galaxy chocolate. When you open the front door, Nina is already in the routine of making dinner. Bossa Nova breezes round the kitchen.

'Did you get the carrots?'

'I did,' and you walk in with the bags, and leave the flowers on the table and put the champagne in the fridge.

'What's all this?'

'Mum's happy we're having the house.'

She comes over and kisses you quickly before going back to one of the pots.

'I'm going to head upstairs and shower.'

'I didn't want to say anything but yeah, better you do that.'

You laugh and go upstairs without telling her what your

grandmother said about the house and the extension. Maybe she's wrong, maybe she's talking about the wrong woman, maybe things will go as planned for once. You can picture yourself in the house, can see Ailish on the floor playing with toys, you can see yourself taking a book from the shelf and leaning down to sit with her, opening it up and saying, let's learn to read? And her smiling, saying, yes, because I'm so big now, and she'll sit on your lap with the book open on her legs and you'll find the letter A and say, that's A, A is for Ailish. A is for Ailish, she'll say. Like me. You'll kiss her on the head and say, yes, you're Ailish. My Ailish. My girl, my girl.

Then

The words the doctors used sounded like something Brigid would learn at school, about bodies in general, diagrams in books, arrows pointing to certain organs, not about her, her body, with her baby boy. She didn't like the prefix of the word: Pre. Preeclampsia. As if there was always more to come, that she wasn't there just yet. Kathleen told her she just needed to rest, not to be listening to much more, just to relax and that the baby would come when it was ready. James came in each day after school and spent the whole weekend with her. He brought homework in with him, asking her a question here and there to get an answer. He brought the poems in, too. Dragging the chair very close to her, he'd almost whisper them, taking so long to get to the end. She remembered how impatient she used to be when he read them, and now, she revelled in the breath and space between the words.

When she was alone, she spoke to Oisín in a way she would write in a diary. In a whisper the words sneaked out of her, and when they took her down darker paths, she would stop talking and let the thoughts just sit with her instead. She became increasingly fearful he would be able to hear her thoughts, that they could taint him somehow.

At night she had one of two dreams. In the first one, she was a shadow, a shadow of a woman not unlike her, pushing a pram along a river. The further she walked the darker it got and the louder the wind became. The trees themselves grew thicker and more ominous. There was a loud crack, a break, and the woman turned, only for a second, so quick that Brigid could not see her face, but in that instant she let go of the pram and the wind took it down a bank and Brigid could see it tumbling into the river.

In the second, she was again this shadow, a form built only from another form, and it was the same woman, and she was late. She held books in both hands and again Brigid could only see her from behind. She was wearing heels and was in a courtyard with old stone buildings surrounding her. Brigid could feel it before the woman, a danger, and before she could call out the woman realized too and quickened her step only to fall, a heel breaking, and she turned and screamed, and before Brigid could see her face, she woke up.

She thought about the dreams during the days, trying to find ways to put them into words, to be able to give voice to them, to try to understand them. In both, she wondered if the woman in her dream was afraid of Brigid herself. If it was Brigid the woman was rushing from. Or was Brigid the woman and if so, what was after her. When she thought about it for too long, she would quickly try to sing a song, or think of her favourite poems, as if art had the power to dissolve, to protect her baby from herself.

Each day that passed brought more physical discomfort and the discomfort leisurely shifted to a humming pain all over her body. It was the middle of the night when she woke with the hot hurt spreading like ripples from her abdomen down through her. The moon was spilling in the window, shining an almost water on the floor so she thought that she was floating. Syrupy moon, what taste would it have? She called out but didn't know if her voice made any sound at all. Had it melted, spooled over windowsill? Calling out again, unable to take her eyes from the moonfloor, thinking that the night, at this very moment, was another planet. She was alone on it. Aloft. The curtain opened around her bed and a foreign light shone on her face and she closed her eyes, and in the gleaming darkness she floated on water, briefly.

Everything was cut short and drawn long. Harsh lights. Sharp sounds. Moonlight in the darkness of her eyes. Alone. A lone lost planet. The opaque azure. The thick aqueous thrill of liquid beneath her feet. Stinging swill at her hips. *My darling, my darling girl.*

Boy? Darling boy?

Shhh, easy now, just stay still.

Still. Moist. A certain light that only shines under the moon. A spool of something, gooey, gunky. Hands reach out. *Just stay like that now, you're all right. No need to push. Don't push now.*

A darkness to the moon.

    Even in the light.

        Even in the thickness of liquid.

            Ripples   and swirls   to a darklight

        a   lightdark.

Flying, is this flying?

Squeaky. No windwhoosh. Metal on metal.

Easy now,

just

      lie

          down.

             My darling   girl

                          girl

Boy?

    Such stillness to the ripples,

        even as they move they are hushed, pacific.

    Floating,

Briefly,   effervescently

                          Forever.

She was split in two. Everything she thought were opposites were just parallels. Madness and sanity. Pain and release. Birth and death. She was on both sides. In the pain she felt a certain anger, an affront to the world. Then there was release and a calmness of letting go. Like letting go of a balloon – it was not the weight she would miss but the memory of holding on. Just when she thought the opposites, the now parallels, would finish her, there was a bald cry, a brilliant frenzy of screaming, and she knew it was him, it was Oisín, and she felt him, briefly in her arms, wet and hot and alive, and then the sound of metal once more, wheels rolling her away from him and she called out, or thought she called out, but her eyes were closing once more and the swelling of the darkness, now complete with no sign of the moon, took over and she fell into it.

When she woke, she was heavy, her body itself felt like a weight and she was surprised to see there was nothing on top of her, no heavy blanket, nothing. Her hands begrudgingly moved to her belly and she knew that it had not been a dream. She turned her head and her mother was sitting on the chair, looking right at Brigid but it took her a few seconds to blink, as if she herself was waking from the same experience. A parallel.

'Oh, Jesus, Bridge.' And she was up and kissing Brigid's face and crying. There was something in that action, of her mother crying that would come back to her. Something Kathleen had unknowingly passed on to her daughter – the eternal worry, the forever uncertainty that only a mother could feel.

'Oisín.' Brigid said. The word now having new stature.

'He's fine. You're both fine. Oh, thank Jesus, Brigid. Oh, my heart.'

'Where?'

'He's in neonatal love, he's fine, he just needs some time. You both do. Oh, Brigid, my darling girl.'

Brigid felt her eyes close once more.

Two days passed and with each hour her strength returned and fragments of what happened came back to her. James spent his time rushing back and forth between the neonatal ward and her bed. Each time with a snippet of information about her baby boy. Bones clicking, which was a good sign, eyes following light, heart rate steady, testicles descended into scrotum. When Oisín was finally brought to her, put into her arms, all the feelings she had had in her life, good or bad, became so distant, as if they belonged to another Brigid, a parallel self.

She looked down at Oisín, and his furrowed little brow and bird-like mouth scared her, or not scared her, but made her feel scared of something she couldn't yet name. She remembered her mother crying. It was the closest she could do to naming what she felt. Oisín, in her arms, was the perfect weight. Her arms, like the rest of her body, had grown a new purpose and she felt incredibly aware of herself and her movements. James stood with one leg against the wall, just like he had so many times, waiting for her to finish her shift at the café, and the love she had for him hurt her now, while at the same time giving her peace. Oisín, she said out loud, my darling, darling boy. And to herself she said, how on earth will I ever be able to protect you?

Now

March is bringing longer days and each evening ends with silence about the planning permission. Your grandmother was right. It was a woman with too much money and nothing to do. Toiling with others for a little kick to her day. It hurt in a sharp way you weren't expecting. You have slowly been moving your things into the small bungalow making it smaller still. Your rent is nearly up and each day you think an answer will come through. It is the waiting that makes it all so frustrating, and knowing there is nothing you can do to get an answer faster, or to get the right answer.

It is Ailish's birthday in a week and you are driving back from the party shop in Mahon Point with bags of party poppers, paper cups and plates, balloons, and other things you cannot name. You let Nina lie in, she's been so tired lately.

You think of all the things you have to get ready for Ailish's day. You have rented the community centre for the afternoon and organized a bouncy castle, music, bubble machine and games.

She was so proud bringing the invitations to crèche, holding them and shuffling them so the edges were all neat. You check your phone to see if any of the parents have RSVP'd. You hope lots of kids show up and wonder how you'll be able to protect her from disappointment, from hurt. At traffic lights, you add to the notes on your phone to pick up orange and blackcurrant cordial.

Back home, Nina is after making poached eggs, and bagels with smoked salmon on a plate, and sourdough bread, and the smell of coffee is welcoming. There is freshly squeezed orange juice. Bossa Nova is playing. Her back is to you when you first go in and it is only when she turns around that you realize how quiet the place is.

'Where's Ailish?'

'Fio took her for a few hours.'

'Really, why?'

'I asked her to.'

'Ok.'

It is then you see the two champagne glasses. It is then she opens the fridge and brings the bottle to the table. You hope it is something about her job, or the planning permission, but you know it isn't and you sit down and take a few heavy breaths. She pours you a glass and it overflows. You get the kitchen roll and lift the glass and one of the plates and soak it up. She pours a little into her glass. She sits across from you and raises her glass and is smiling with her eyebrows raised.

'Well, fuck me.' You say and laugh a little. 'Jesus, I was not expecting that.'

'I know,' she says and you can see it all over her. The pure bliss of it.

'When did you find out?'

'Last week but I thought I was.'

'Have you been to the doctor?'

'Nope, just the home tests.'

'Jesus. Ok, fuck, ok.' Your eyes flitter around the room and you cannot think of a concrete thought. But you are smiling. Ok, you think. Yes, why the fuck not. Yes. And you think of Ailish being a big sister, and something like an old painting is in your mind, the brushstrokes too thick, but she is there, on a chair holding a baby, with a big sister smile on her face.

'You're happy?' she asks.

'Yeah,' you say, 'I think I am. Floored like, but yeah, think this is good. It's good, right?'

'It's amazing. I didn't even know how much I wanted it.'

You both stand up and already you are careful not to hug her too tight. Already the thoughts of what can go wrong are inking themselves to the forefront of your mind. A baby. Ok, you think. You want to tell your mother immediately and break away from Nina.

'We should visit my mum, tell her.'

'Of course. Now?'

'Well, no, like let's eat and then we can go?'

'Ok, let's just relax a little.'

'I know, I just worry…'

'I know you do. It's ok.'

You are hugging again and then you both sit down. You drain the glass and pour another. Drain that and poor one more.

'Right then, another baby!'

Nina laughs. 'Ailish will be the best big sister.'

'She will. We really need to build that fucking extension now.'

'I know. I've been thinking about that, too. I know it'll be tight but even if we don't get the planning, it'll still be ours, it will still be a home.'

'Yeah, you might be right.'

'I've got some more ideas for the smaller bedroom.'

'Really? Ok, wow. You've thought this through. Jesus.'

'I know.' She's got that goofy grin and you can see her trying to tighten it, make it smaller.

'Right, let's eat!'

You both pick at the food. You drink more of the champagne, enough to be a little tipsy and giddy. It is only 10.45 so you decide against more.

'I can't wait to call my parents,' she says.

'Call them!'

'They're still asleep.'

'Oh yeah.'

'Let's go visit your mum and then we can call them. Fiona said she'd take Ailish until nap time.'

'Does Fio know?'

'No, but she suspects something.'

'Ok, just 'cos I know they're trying, too. So let's not tell them yet.'

'Of course. How are they?'

You relay what Fio has told you. How it took her a while to want to try again and how difficult it's been.

'It's so hard. Remember us?' She looks out the window.

'I do.'

'I've been thinking about him, you know, since I found out. How Ailish wouldn't be here if what happened hadn't happened, how this baby wouldn't be. And still I think I'd change it all, you know, to not have gone through that.'

'I know. I can't imagine what it was like for you.'

'It's weird. I only have flashes, you know. There was so much blood and then everything is more feelings than actual memories.

I still felt him. I could still feel him, even when they took him out of me. For so long I felt him inside of me.'

'You're amazing.'

You want to change the conversation, not because you don't want to talk about it but don't want to remember this moment of a new baby and always have the thought of what wasn't. The image of the jar.

'Let's get ready?' She says, already standing up. Smiling again, but softer now, a betrayal of sorts.

'Yeah, come on preggers,' and you link her arm and you go up the stairs together.

Your mother is sitting in the armchair by the window when you arrive. She has a knitted blanket over her legs and a plate next to her with the peels of an eaten orange. Nina is first over to her and leans down to take her hand.

'How are you feeling Brigid?'

'Oh, just tired.' She responds and smiles at Nina.

You sit down on the bed and Nina sits on the chair by the table.

'Has Gran been in today?'

'But of course,' and you turn to see your grandmother at the door, one hand out as if holding a tray, a droll smile on her face. In that image of her, you can see what she thinks she must look like and what she actually looks like. The pose is a little farcical and her body is too small and frail to really support it.

'Carolina, you look magnificent as always. What you're doing with him, I'll never know.'

She laughs and sits on the bed.

'Someone's missing,' your mother says and she picks up the plate and puts it on her lap, wringing the orange peel through her fingers.

'Ailish, is it, mum? She's with Fio. Remember Fiona, my friend?'

'No, no, someone else. You didn't bring him?' She looks at Nina, now breaking the orange peel into little pieces on the plate. Nina smiles a little and leans down and takes the plate from her and places it on the locker, then holds your mother's hands, lifting her up to stand and, still holding your mother's hands, puts them softly on her belly.

'He's here, Brigid, he's here.'

You see your mother smile a little as she moves her hands gently across Nina's belly. Your grandmother's hand slips into yours and when you turn to her, she is smiling softly, her eyes closed. She whispers just enough for you to hear, *what a moment to be alive*.

You walk over to your mother and take one of her hands, and Nina is holding the other.

'My darling boy,' she says. Your arm brings her into you, her on one side, Nina on the other, and your grandmother slips in with her arm around Nina. A little semi-circle of what was, what is, and what will be. There is something there, just outside memory, and for once you let it be, just that, a floating flotsam of the past, drifting out of sight. To be in a moment, completely, you think, like this, now, is the essence of living, and if only it could be taught, or if only you could learn it, like an alphabet, and repeat it over and over to music, so each moment that passes would be whole and you could live it entirely, swallowing the sounds of it, the tastes and nuances of it, then you could stop whatever it is that draws you into the dredges of memory, taking you further and further away from now.

'Well, enough of that,' your grandmother says, 'have you thought of names?'

Now

The nurse doesn't stop talking, telling Brigid about the weather outside, and how Oisín is on his way up, and how excited she must be. I chose these pants and your gold sandals, she says, lifting Brigid up into a sitting position on the bed. She looks familiar to Brigid, Gwen's sister maybe, what was her name?

'Are you Gwen's sister? My apologies, your name is gone from me.'

'Oh, no. No sisters me. The only girl and seven brothers!'

'Oh, sounds messy.'

'Ha! It sure was.'

'You're so like Gwen, the same eyes. Soft. Lovely eyes.'

'Thanks, Brigid. Now come on, Oisín will be here soon.'

'We nearly had a boy, that would have been his name, Oisín. A still birth in the end.'

'Come on, Brigid, you're ok. You're just mixing some things up. Stand up now, there you go. It's a lovely day out. I chose this nice linen top for you, what do you think?'

Brigid doesn't say anything but lets the woman lift her hands up and pull her nightie from her and put the top over her head and find her hands to pull through the holes. The nurse sprays perfume on Brigid's neck and on the inside of her wrists and the smell is sweet and flowery.

'Is my mammy here? It smells of my mammy.'

The nurse goes silent and turns around. She holds the sides of the sink for a second before standing back up.

'Now, you look lovely. Would you like a little bit of lipstick? Yeah, go on. Hold on.'

The nurse takes a pale purple from her own bag, the colour that raspberries might leave on a napkin, and curves it round Brigid's thin lips.

'Like this, Brigid,' and the nurse slaps and punches her lips together making a popping sound. Brigid copies and laughs.

'And you'll see the little one, he must be the cutest baby I've ever seen,'

'Who's that? Yours is it?'

'No, no, your grandson, Brigid. You're going out for the day, remember? Oisín is coming, they've got the house sorted? You're spending the day there, remember?'

'Babies are so small. You forget that don't you, how small they are?'

'You do. Well, he loves you anyway, does Tommy. Lights up when he sees you.'

'Are my parents here then, I can smell my mammy.'

'No, no, love. Tommy is your grandson, darling little thing. Oisín is coming to collect you, you're going to spend the day with them.'

'Oh, oh.'

Brigid looks at her lap, she puts her right hand on her left

The Language of Remembering

hand, then her left on her right, switching over and over.

'You haven't seen Gwen at all have you?'

'I haven't, love. Come on now. I know it's a lot, let's sit down there. I'll bring in some breakfast.'

She helps Brigid into the armchair and places a photo album on her lap with the pages open. It's new and smells of new and the photos are of Oisín and Nina, Ailish and Tommy. And as she turns the pages over she sees her own house, the bungalow, and each photo shows it changing in some way, walls being removed and others being added on, until it is higher, with more windows, and it is painted, and Oisín is standing in front of it, with Nina to his right and Ailish is at Nina's legs, and Oisín is holding a little baby, swathed in blue. She gets to the end of the book and starts again, the faces becoming more familiar, a story there in the shadows and pockets of her mind.

The nurse comes back with some tea, toast and two boiled eggs and helps Brigid with the spoon and the fork.

'It'll be your first time at the house then?'

'Yes, yes, it looks lovely. I think it was mine.'

'It was, Brigid. Remember, you and James lived there.'

'Yes. It was nice to get there, you know, to get close to the sea.'

'Oh, it's a lovely spot down there.'

'Is my mammy around at all, I think I might have missed her. Kathleen is her name. I think she might have been here a minute ago.'

'Come on now, love, eat up for me. There you go.'

When she has finished a slice of toast and one of the eggs the nurse takes the tray and leaves, and Brigid looks out the window. Oisín is coming to collect me for the day, she thinks. Oisín is coming to collect me for the day. Oisín is coming. Oisín. Oisín, my darling boy. And outside the window, in the garden, is a woman standing beneath a large silver birch, she seems restless and picks at the bark. Ah, there she is, Brigid thinks, mammy is here, I knew it. I'll have to tell Oisín she's waiting, he knows how she can get. I'll have to tell Oisín, she thinks, he's coming to get me today, Oisín is coming, my darling, darling boy.

She looks out the window for a long time without moving. The woman from underneath the tree walks away and Bridgid follows her with her eyes thinking her rather elegant. A refined woman that looks nothing like her mother. She does not think of her mother now. A rhythm plays in her mind, high pitched and slow, da de da de da da, she says in her mind, to the rhythm that spills out. She looks down at her hands and feels outside herself, she moves them to make sure they are not some dead props placed upon her lap, and they are reluctant and stiff, and she laughs a little, looking at the fingers go in and out of each other, curling at the knuckles.

There is a noise outside. Something has fallen. She looks outside the window once more, expectantly. The garden is long and wide, and the shrubs make a wall of themselves, reaching upwards, and there is a large tree. It is familiar. She has seen it before. She looks around the room, not sure of where she is. Or if she is meant to be there. She tries to stand up, but it is difficult, and she falls back in the chair and she hears a quiet release of air. There is a large tree outside the window. She remembers her father pushing her around in something, or maybe it was a bike. She remembers the air on her face. Or a car. James. Driving so fast. She turns around expecting her sitting room and is unsure of the objects that take up such little space, so sparsely. She looks at the bed in the corner of the room. She thinks she is visiting someone, but where are they? She turns to see where they might be and notices a large tree in the garden. It reminds her of something.

There is a quick low knock at the door and she thinks, ah, James is here. A man walks into the room, the same long limbs as James, the same features. How he's changed.

'James?'

'It's me mum!'

And he shifts into focus for a quick second, a history in his cheekbones.

'My lovely boy!'

And then he walks towards her and is talking but she can't take in what he is saying as she is suddenly quite scared but of what she cannot say.

'It's ok, it's ok, let's take your time,' the man's voice is saying. It sounds familiar. There is a slight lisp to it she once knew. A lilt. She tries to speak as she feels herself lifted to her feet. The man's arms are around her and she feels safe.

'A dhaid, bhraitheas uaim thú.'

'It's me, mum, don't worry, you'll be fine.'

She walks, or rather, she is walked and the door opens in front of her and then there is a hall that causes a slight fuzz in her mind, and then another door, and then she is outside and the lovely air whispers at her neck, and the noise of cars skid on gravel, and birds squawk hurriedly, and there is a dog barking. Inside the car there is music playing and she starts to sing along. She closes her eyes as the car rattles, and she is at the kitchen table with her mammy and her daddy. He is singing, using the edge of the table for his fingers to steady a beat, and her mammy is humming in a higher pitch, and Brigid sings out the chorus with him. The smell of the house alive inside of her. When she opens her eyes the trees pass her by.

'You've such a nice voice, mum.'

She turns and looks at the man driving. Her boy, a man now.

But the same look about him, the same slant of the nose, the same smiling eyes.

'We're going to the house, mum, I hope you like it. Did you like the album I made, so you can see the progress?'

'I loved it, oh it's lovely.' She says, although she doesn't know what he means but there's such a lovely tone to his voice, such a lightness in it that she doesn't want it to change. Any of it.

'Oh, good. I hope you like it now, I really do.'

'I will, I'm sure I will.' She says, wondering what it is she might like. The song finishes and another starts. The melody makes Brigid want her mammy.

'Will mammy be there?' She asks, looking at the man who just a second ago was her son, and now is not.

'Nina will, and the kids, Ailish can't wait to see you. And you can hold Tommy. You might sing to him, it always helps him sleep.'

'I will, I will of course,' she says, thinking again of her daddy, the way they'd sing together. As the car parks up, she sees the house. It is Oisín's house, she knows that, but at the same time it is hers, and it is James beside her, bringing her there for the first time, telling her, we don't need my parents, we don't need that house, we can buy our own, and it is there, the house by the sea, and James is opening the door for her, helping her out and her whole life is ahead of her, and Oisín will be happy here, she thinks. He'll be happy here by the sea.

'We'll be happy here, won't we?' She says, walking next to him.

'We will, we'll be really happy.'

She smiles and they walk to the front door, and she knows, inside of herself, that it will open out a new future, and that James is right, they will be happy here.

Acknowledgements

I'd like to start by thanking those who guided and inspired me from a young age, especially Eileen McCollum who left us not too long ago, for showing me the wonder of words, and Colette Murphy, the best teacher anyone could ask for. To my parents, my brothers and sister, for giving me more material than I'll ever be able to use – I love you all dearly. To my amazing friends for bigging me up while keeping me grounded, I couldn't have got this far without ye.

To the amazing writing community in Ireland who have helped me hugely, especially The Munster Literature Centre for all they do for emerging writers. Thanks to Danny Denton for a Mentorship in 2021. I'm very grateful to have worked with Alexander MacLeod in 2023, whose writing and mentorship inspired me to no end. To the Arts Council Ireland for an Agility Award in 2022.

To Lucy Holme and Rosie Morris for all their support, chats, workshopping and laughter – so happy our paths crossed. To Stephen Brophy, there's no one else I'd like to spend hours debating em dashes and en dashes with – thank you for your comments on this book and for your friendship. To all my writer friends for the chats, pints, laughter and shared frustrations: Daragh Fleming, Fiona Ennis, Laura Cassidy, Sean Tanner, Cat Hogan, and Sean Hewitt. To Joanne McCarthy, for helping me with the Irish, and so many other things on this writing journey. Special thanks to Mary O' Donnell for her guidance and belief – so happy we met all that time ago in São Paulo.

To Paul McVeigh and everyone involved in the residency I received in 2023 – this was one of the most inspiring and productive weeks of my life and greatly improved this book. To the Irish Writers' Centre for selecting me in the Evolution Programme, 2024 – the most amazing experience so far. To John Kenny and Elaine Feeney at the University of Galway, for the opportunity and the kindness.

To my incredible agent Eleanor Birne for believing in, and sticking with, me. To Sean Campbell and everyone at époque press for taking a chance and making this the best book it could be.

To Aurora and Luna Faye, my two brilliant daughters who make all this worthwhile – I'll never have enough words to tell you both how much I love you. And finally, to Cí, o maior amor da minha vida, nada disso seria possível sem ti.